W9-COV-972

GUNMEN AHEAD!

Well, our stage was bouncing along on that god damned rough old road and rolling down into a kind of valley with clumps of trees here and there along the sides and some piles of boulders and such, and I had old Marlin handcuffed by his left wrist to the rails what run around the top to keep the baggage in place, and I was setting there right behind him with my Winchester in my hand. I was trying to watch all around, up ahead, on both sides and behind us, but I wasn't keeping up with all that too good. I noticed that old Ash Face, he didn't move his head at all. He was just watching right up in front of us. Of a sudden I heard him yell.

"Barjack," he said. "Straight ahead."

Well, I swung around to look, and sure enough, there they was all strung out across the road. They was four of them, all right and right away I figgered it had to be them four members of old Snake Eyes's gang. Two of them was holding six guns ready, and two was holding rifles.

"Keep them rolling," I yelled. I knowed that Ash Face and Goose Neck made pretty good targets up there on the box, but that's how come we was counting on old Jug Marlin being a kind of deterrent up on top. I grabbed Jug by the hair of his head and pulled him up tall and shoved him kind of between Ash Face and Goose Neck.

"Show yourself, god damn you," I yelled into the side of his head.

I levelled my Winchester. . . .

Other *Leisure* books by Robert J. Conley:
BARJACK
THE ACTOR
INCIDENT AT BUFFALO CROSSING
BACK TO MALACHI

BROKE LOOSE

ROBERT J. CONLEY

LEISURE BOOKS NEW YORK CITY

A LEISURE BOOK®

August 2000

Published by

Dorchester Publishing Co., Inc.
276 Fifth Avenue
New York, NY 10001

If you purchased this book without a cover you should be aware that this book is stolen property. It was reported as "unsold and destroyed" to the publisher and neither the author nor the publisher has received any payment for this "stripped book."

Copyright © 2000 by Robert J. Conley

All rights reserved. No part of this book may be reproduced or transmitted in any form or by any electronic or mechanical means, including photocopying, recording or by any information storage and retrieval system, without the written permission of the Publisher, except where permitted by law.

ISBN 0-8439-4756-X

The name "Leisure Books" and the stylized "L" with design are trademarks of Dorchester Publishing Co., Inc.

Printed in the United States of America.

BROKE LOOSE

Chapter One

I was setting by the front window of the new and snitzy White Owl Supper Club on the main street of Asininity just sipping at a morning cup of coffee when I seen the two of them ride in just bigger than hell. One of them was a total stranger, and I could see even from that distance that his hands was tied behind his back, but the other one was by God old Happy Bonapart hisself. Happy was the one son of a bitch in the whole entire damned world that I was most anxious to see again, but I never thought even in my most precious dreams that I would really ever be that lucky. I wanted to see old Happy so bad because the little runt had run out on me once, back then when I'd had all that trouble with the goddamned Bensons, and I had swore at that time that if I ever was so fortunate as to see him again, even if I was ninety goddamned years old, I would knock the holy snot out of him right then and there without even first saying howdy.

I sure was happy to see ole Happy, also 'cause Asininity had growed pretty tame and quiet, and I was getting almighty bored most to death with my new life as the lazy-ass marshal of a sleepy town and a businessman and a husband and a daddy to a little brat. My poor little ole Lillian had popped out a pair a twins, one of each, but we had done lost the little gal. Now, I know it ain't likely to endear me none to anyone out there, calling my own little surviving son a brat, but damn it all to hell, he surely was just that. Likely Lillian had spoiled him all the worser because a the little gal. Hell, I don't know, but he was for sure a snot-nosed, dirty-assed little brat what got ever damn thing he ever wanted just his own peculiar little way, and that was all because a his damn prissy mama. My Lillian, what I had fell deep in love with 'cause she was the goddamndest lady I had ever seen in my whole entire life a travels and wild-ass adventures, had turned out to be a ring-tailed bitch as a wife.

Hell, I had even begun to think that maybe poor old Texas Jack, rest his old soul, had been right about her way back then whenever I had shot him dead when I found the two of them smooching it up right smack in my own office chair. She nagged at me something fierce all the damn time, and she absolute spoiled that little brat something terrible. Other than that, she just pranced and prissed around in the White Owl just like as if she was in San Francisco or some other such hot damn place. And the goddamned place was way too fancy for Asininity. It never did have much business.

Whenever I could manage to break myself loose from Lillian, I spent my time back at Harvey's Hooch House, where I felt right comfy, and I even tuck up with old Bonnie Boodle again at least ever' now and then. Bonnie even seemed to forget that she had tried to kill me more than once over Lillian. I think that Lillian knowed what was going on too, but she just didn't really give a damn.

So anyhow, I was real happy to see old Happy. I needed me some kind of a diversion, and I had felt like I wanted to hit someone real bad for quite a spell. I noticed out the window that old Happy had pulled up right smack dab in front of the marshaling office and him leading that there other feller with his hands tied behind his back. Happy had dismounted and was lapping the reins of the horses around the hitching rail there. I slurped down my coffee, burning my throat and gullet some, and went out the door, headed for my marshaling office.

I was stepping down off the board sidewalk into the damn muddy street when Happy tried the office door and found it locked. He turned around to look up and down the street, and then he seen me coming. He walked on toward me kind of tentative-like. It had been a long time. We was about to meet there in the middle of the street, and he grinned real wide, like I'd seen him grin a thousand times before, and he stuck out his hand toward me, and he said, "Barjack—"

But that was all he said, 'cause right then I smacked him a good one right up to the side of his jaw. It felt great, and it give a good loud smacking sound too, and old Happy's head snapped around, and he fell right over splat in the mud. He looked up at me, and what a look he had on his face. He should ought to have expected that from me after he done what he done, but I guess he never. He rubbed the side of his jaw with a muddy hand. "What the hell was that for?" he said.

"You run out on me in my greatest hour of need," I said, "and I swore that I would do that the next time I seen you."

"You told me to kill Bonnie," he said. "I couldn't do that."

"Well, get up out of the goddamned street," I said. "Folks're looking at us."

I didn't offer him no hand, though, 'cause he was all over muddy as hell, and I didn't want to get no mud on me, other than on my old boots where it already was. "What the hell you doing back here, anyway?" I asked him. He slipped a time or two, but he finally got on up to his feet.

"I brung you a prisoner, Barjack," he said.

"Well," I said, "I'll go lock the son of a bitch in jail. You go get yourself cleaned up and meet me over in the Hooch House. You can tell me who he is over there."

I went on over to the office and unlocked the door. Then I went out in the street again right there beside the prisoner what was still just setting there on the horse, and I reached up and tuck hold of his shirt-sleeve and dragged him down out of his saddle. He like to have fell in the mud.

"Hey," he said.

"Shut up and watch your ass," I said. "Come on." I jerked on him and tuck him on inside and shoved him into a jail cell. Then I shut the door and locked it. He turned around and give me a hell of a look.

He was a tall lanky feller, ugly as hell, and he was dressed like a cowhand. He had sandy hair and he needed a shave real bad, but the thing what struck me most about his looks was his little slit snake eyes.

"You going to untie my hands?" he said.

"I never tied them," I said.

"What the hell kind of way to lock a man up is this?" he said.

"Turn around," I said, and he turned his back to me and kind of reached his tied hands out so I could get to them. I tuck hold of his shirt collar and jerked on it, banging his head against the bars. He yowled out real good, and then I shoved hard and he sprawled out on the floor. He twisted his head around to look at me.

"Don't go hollering around at me in my own goddamned jailhouse," I said. "I don't like it, and I won't put up with it." Then I walked on out of the office and headed over for Harvey's. It was still too early for old Bonnie to have got her fat ass out of bed, so I never seen her, and it was a little early for whiskey drinking, but then being there in the Hooch House I couldn't hardly help myself. I told old Aubrey Waldrip to bring me two glasses and a bottle. I knowed that Happy would be along soon enough. I set down

11

at a table and poured myself about three fingers of whiskey and waited.

When old Happy showed up at last, he had cleaned hisself up and changed his clothes, and I'd already had myself about three drinks, I guess. He stopped a good ten feet away from the table, looking kind of tentative.

"You going to hit me again?" he said.

"Hell, no," I said. "I promised myself that I'd do it, and I done it. That's all. Come on over here and set." He come over and pulled out a chair and set down in it, and I poured the extra glass full of whiskey and shoved it at him.

"It's kind of early," he said.

"Aw hell," I said, "drink it up. We ain't seen each other in a spell."

Happy tuck hisself a drink then. I knowed from the old days that he could handle it. 'Course, he couldn't handle it as good as me, but then I never knowed many who could. "What you been up to, Happy?" I asked him.

"Aw, just knocking around here and there," he said.

"You shouldn't have run out on me," I said. "You had yourself a good job and throwed it away." He tuck a sip of whiskey, looking at me from over the top of his glass. Then he put down the glass.

"You know why I run out," he said.

"Yeah, well," I said, "I guess I'm just as glad that you never killed old Bonnie after all." Then I grinned and kind of leaned over the table toward him and said real low-like, "You know, me and her's taken to screwing each other again now and then."

"Barjack," Happy said, like he was astonished and maybe a little bit horrified, "you got yourself a wife now."

"Yeah," I said, "and a damn kid, and the two of them's about to make me crazy." I picked up my glass and drank it down, then poured myself another. "Drink up," I said to Happy. "Hell, I'm way ahead of you." Happy tuck another drink, but he never drank it all down. 'Course, I had poured his glass pretty damn full.

"Barjack," he said, "that prisoner I brought you—"

"The hell with him," I said. "We'll talk about him later. Right now we're going to set here and talk about old times and get drunk. We're two old friends that ain't seen each other for a while. I don't want to talk business."

He finished off his drink and shoved the glass on over at me. I poured it full again and poured myself another one. It come to me just then that the last time I seen old Happy I was drunk on my ass. That was the night I had been so drunk that I had knowed I wouldn't be able to defend myself, and I had knowed that old Bonnie was wanting to kill me, and I had told Happy that if he was to spot her coming at me to just shoot her dead. That was the reason he had run out on me. Well, that was all in the past, and I had punched him for it, so that episode was done wrapped up. I always had liked old Happy anyhow, and I was glad to have him back.

"You staying in town, Happy?" I asked him.

"I reckon not," he said. "I got no job here. I just come in to deliver that prisoner to you is all, so when we get that took care of, I'll move along, I guess."

Well, I didn't want old Happy running off too soon, 'cause I didn't really have no good buddies in town, and I kind of liked having him back around, so I figgered I could just delay getting that all tuck care of for a while. I said, "Happy, old partner, is that there son of a bitch a real legitimate prisoner?"

"He's a wanted man, Barjack," Happy said. "That's why the hell I brought him on over here."

"Well, then," I said, "I reckon the town can put you up till we get his paperwork all done right and proper. It might could take a few days, you know."

Old Happy tossed hisself down another drink. It looked like he was actual trying to catch up with me. He was a pretty fair drinker, but I knowed that he would get wildcat-ass drunk if he tried to catch up to me, and I thought that it just might be a whole hell of a lot of fun to let him try it. I poured us each another one. "Happy, you old son of a bitch," I said, "I'm glad to see you."

He rubbed his jaw where I had busted him earlier. "Well," he said, "I guess I'm glad to see you, too, after all."

"I'm sorry about that jaw-busting I give you," I said, "but I had to do it. I had swore I would, and I had promised myself I would, and if I hadn't done it, I wouldn't never have been able to look myself in the face again. You understand?"

"Yeah," he said. "I understand. A swearing is a thing you can't ignore."

'Bout then old Bonnie come a-flouncing down the stairs, her great huge tits just a-bouncing up and down. She had done applied her face paint, she never showed herself without that, but I could still see the dark circles underneath her eyes. She seen me, and then she seen old Happy setting there with me, and she grinned real big and come a-running. Happy seen her coming, and being a real gentleman, he stood up, and I seen that his old legs was already getting a bit rubbery.

The way them two come together, I figgered the impact of Bonnie's mass would have killed him, but it never. They just throwed their arms around each other and whirled around and around like they was dancing. "Oh, Happy," Bonnie said, kind of gurgling. "Happy, it's so good to see you." Happy opined as how it was good to see her too, and finally they broke it up and he set back down, and Bonnie stuck a chair between the two of us and set her broad ass end down on it.

"What brings you back to town, Happy?" Bonnie asked him.

"We ain't talking about that," I said. "What brung him in is business, and we ain't talking no business, not just yet. We're old friends having a good time together. That's all." I started to yell at old Aubrey to bring a glass for Bonnie, but Aubrey knowed Bonnie and her habits better than any of us, and he was already practical at the table with her glass and her own favorite brand of hooch. He put it on the table in front of her.

"Thanks, Aubrey," she said. "All right. No business. So what do we talk about? Hey, this feels like the good old days, the three of us here like this."

"But it ain't the good old days," I said. "I've got that goddamned house over there and Lillian and that kid in it, and after a while when she finds out that I been setting here getting drunk as a skunk with old friends this early in the day, she's going to lay into me like the great mother god of all tongues."

Bonnie give me a hell of a look. "You made your goddamned bed, Barjack," she said. "Now you got to sleep in it."

"Yeah," I said, grinning, "but I get to sleep in your bed, too, ever' now and then, don't I, sweet thighs?"

"Oh, shut up, you old fart," she said.

Drunk as he was getting already, I seen old Happy blush a little at that talk. He always did embarrass easy. He was kind of tender, you know. "Happy," I said, "what's wrong with you, little pard? That there bedroom talk make you horny? Hell, old Bonnie will take you upstairs and do you a hell of a good turn, won't you, Bonnie?"

"That ain't no way to talk in front of a lady, Barjack," Happy said.

"Well, by God," I said, "I apologize all to hell. Why the hell don't you two go on upstairs and get safe away from old Barjack's uncouth bull? Hell, it's a celebration anyhow, ain't it? Well, go celebrate."

Old Bonnie give me a hell of a look, and by God, she just jumped up and shoved me and my chair both over on our backs, and of course I had my whiskey glass in my hand, and so I slopped whiskey all over myself. The only thing that bothers me about slopping whiskey all over myself is that it's wasted that way. It should have gone in me rather than on me. Well, that kind of knocked my wind out, and I banged my head on the goddamned floor, but I could still see straight, and I seen Bonnie grab hold of old Happy by his arm and pull him up to his feet. Then she turned and give me another of them looks, and she said, "You think we won't? Well, by God we will. Come on, Happy." And damned if she didn't lead that old boy right on up the stairs. Well, I couldn't help myself. I just laid there on my back, and when my wind come around again, I commenced to laughing.

Old Aubrey come ambling on over and helped me back up and got me seated at the table again, and he poured me out a fresh drink into my glass. "You all right now, Barjack?" he said.

"Hell yes," I said. "Old Bonnie, she was just making a statement is all. If she was really mad, she wouldn't have pushed me. She'd have hit me, and she'd have hit me with something damn hard."

Bonnie and Happy was gone for a spell, and all I can assume is that she was really bouncing him all over her bed, but it was kind of hard to imagine. Whenever I tried to picture it, you know, get a real image in my mind of what was going on up there, the only thing I could see was poor old Happy's face getting all red while Bonnie pulled down his britches. But I figured there's likely to be a heap of difference in the way a man reacts out in public to bedroom talk with a woman present, and how he reacts once she's got him alone upstairs in her own for real bedroom. Anyhow, I hoped that she was really giving him a bang up for real what for up there, and I was in a position to know that she could do it.

I amused myself for as long as I could by trying to picture Bonnie and Happy up there nekkid in bed together, and then I begun to get some bored with my own company. I got up, picked up my bottle in one hand and my glass in the other, and kind of staggered just a little over to the bar. "Hey, Aubrey," I said. It wasn't busy at all in the Hooch House that time of day, and so old Aubrey come right over to see what it was I was wanting. "Do you think old Happy's on top up yonder, or you reckon sweet Bonnie's riding on him?"

"I got no idea, Barjack," Aubrey said. "The only thing I know is that you're getting mighty drunk awful early in the day. Miss Lillian ain't going to like it."

"Happy's back," I said. "I'm celebrating. That's all. To hell with Lillian. She ain't the goddamned Queen of Sheba. Is she?"

"I don't know, Barjack," Aubrey said, "but the last time I recall you celebrating like this, poor old Billy Brown got his arm broke, Charlie Simmons just up and disappeared, Ace Malloy's dog got killed, and this place didn't have a single chair nor table without at least one broken leg."

"Aw, stop worrying, Aubrey," I said. "I ain't going to start no trouble. Hell, I'm the goddamned marshal. I'm supposed to stop trouble, ain't I?"

"S'posed to," Aubrey said, but I didn't really like the way he said it, the silly little bastard. And I kind of told him so. Well, at least I called him that. I said, "You silly little bastard." Just about then Bonnie and Happy come back down the stairs, and I wasn't yet too drunk to see the look on Happy's face. He was looking a bit sheepish, you know, like he had done it all right, and he knowed that me and Aubrey knowed that he had done it, but he wished that we didn't know. Old Bonnie, on the other hand, she had her head held up high. She was lording it over me. Taking in the looks on both their faces, I knowed that they had enjoyed themselves a damn good romp.

I stepped out away from the bar to meet Happy, and I was wobbly, but I was smiling at him. I'm always happy for a friend when he's had a damn good time. "Well, Happy," I said, "you old son of a bitch, did old Bonnie do you right?"

And then I'll be a bandy-legged bastard son of an ugly old range cow if Happy didn't draw back and give me a hard roundhouse right to the jaw that knocked me clean off my feet and rolled me backwards right over the goddamned bar. When I come down on the other side, I fell into Aubrey and bowled him over too. I reached up and tuck hold of the edge of the bar with both my hands and pulled till my eyes was peeping over at Happy and Bonnie over on the other side.

"Barjack," Happy said, "how many times I got to tell you that ain't no way to talk in front of a lady?"

"Hell," I said, standing on up, "I didn't think it would matter none, considering what you two just done with each other."

I tried to get my right leg up on top of the bar to crawl back over on the proper side. I don't know why I didn't just walk down to the end and around, but I didn't. I was trying to crawl over, and old Aubrey, he give me a hand. He shoved on my leg till we got it up on the bar, and then he shoved on my ass, and pretty soon I was laying on top of the bar on my belly. I slipped my both legs on over and dropped down to the floor. I stood there weaving some for a minute or two, and I shook my head a little trying to clear it.

"I'm sorry I had to do that to you, Barjack," Happy said, "but it really galls me something awful when you talk like that in front of Bonnie."

"Aw, hell," I said, kind of ducking my head a little, "it didn't really hurt me none." And then while I had him off guard like that, I tuck another quick swing at him, and it was a good one, too. I popped him right square on the chin, and he fell hard back on top of the nearest table, and the legs give out under it, and the tabletop with Happy laid across it crashed hard on down to the floor.

It was Happy's turn to try to shake his fuzzy head clear. He shuck it. Then he got up real slow. He stood there looking quizzical at me for just a bit. Then he raised up his little knobby fists in front of his face, all ready to have a goddamned fair fistfight. I hauled off and kicked him in the crotch.

Chapter Two

Well, by God, I don't rightly know what all happened after that, but it was way after a while, I could tell, that I woke up right there in a cell in my own damn jail. I was just laying there on the hard, cold cell floor, and old Happy, he was stretched out on the cot, and he was still out cold. I set up groaning and kind of shuck my head a little bit to clear some of the fuzziness out of it and then looked around. We was in the next-door cell to the one Happy's prisoner was locked up in, and I seen that the iron-bars door to the cell we was in was standing wide open. I figured that me and old Happy had either knocked each other out or quit fighting and started up drinking again and passed out, and then someone had just hauled our old sorry asses on over to the jailhouse to sleep it off. I wondered for just a bit who it was what might have done us that kindness, but then, I guessed I really didn't give a damn. I started in trying to get up on my feet, and then the son of a bitch in the next-door cell seen that I was still alive, and he commenced to haranguing on me once again.

"Hey, Marshal," he said. "You sorry son of a bitch, I'm still tied up here, and I ain't et since that bastard got the drop on me. Not one bite. And both of my hands from my wrists on down have gone plumb to sleep, and now they're tingling something awful. You starve and torture your prisoners in this here jail? Is that a common practice in this sorry-ass goddamned town?"

"If you just stop farting out your mouth," I said, "I might consider taking a little better care of you in just a while. On the other damn hand, if I hear one more nagging, complaining word out of your ass, I'm going to act like as if I plumb forgot that you're even in there. You hear me now?"

I reckon that there comment soaked in pretty good into his ugly head all right, 'cause he didn't say nothing more, not just then. I stood on up and straightened myself some, and then it sudden come on me that I needed me some food my own damn self, and I could sure as hell use me another drink to finish up the clearing out of my head. I looked over there at old Happy, but he didn't appear to me to be wanting much else out of life just then other than just sleep, so I decided to let him be for a spell, and, without thinking too much about it, I walked on over to the White Owl.

Lillian seen me just as soon as I come walking in

the front door. It was kind of between the lunch time and the supper time by then, so there wasn't hardly no customers in the damn place. 'Course, there wasn't never too many in there, even in the busy times. There was always more over at the Hooch House. Hell, you could get yourself a good steak over there, too, and you didn't have to act so fancy for it. You could go into the Hooch House with mud on your boots or blood on your face and just about any damn way you might please. Then, if you was to want to go upstairs with a woman, why, if you was too nasty, she'd just order up a bath for you, and you'd have to get yourself cleaned up some before you could crawl in between her sheets, but that was about it. I don't know why in hell I went into the White Owl instead of the Hooch House. The only excuse I can think of for my dumb-ass self is that I was still a bit woozy and wasn't thinking any too damn straight. Anyhow, old Lillian come right straight at me with her eyes a-blazing.

"Barjack," she snapped out, "you look like hell. Just what do you mean coming in here like that? And what have you been up to, anyway?"

"Aw, hell, lovey," I said, "we just been having us a welcome-home celebration is all. Old Happy Bonapart come back to town."

"Happy? And you were celebrating?" she said. "I thought you were going to punch him right in the jaw the next time you saw him."

"Well, I done that," I said, "and then with that out of the way, we got to celebrating. I come in here 'cause I need me a glass of whiskey and a good steak dinner. That's what I come over here for."

"Well, where's Happy?" she asked.

"He's over yonder in the jail," I said.

"You didn't lock him up, did you?" she asked me.

"No, hell, I never done that. He's just sleeping it off in a cell is all," I said. "The door ain't even locked. He can get up and go out whenever he takes a notion to. Now, how about that whiskey and steak?"

"You're not a real customer in here," she said. "You can pour your own damn whiskey. I'll go tell Horace to start cooking your lunch."

"Tell him to be damn quick about it, too," I said, trying to get back some of my manliness there in front of her back, and as Lillian headed on for the kitchen to put old Horace to work on my steak, I walked on over to the bar and around to the back side of it. I found myself a bottle of good brown whiskey and poured me a tumbler full. I never did like to use them damn little bitty shot glasses but just only to sell whiskey in to someone else. I stood there behind the bar and tuck me a nice drink and felt my head starting to clear up, and then I filled the tumbler back up. I walked on out again to the eating area and plopped myself down in a chair at a table to wait for my meal. I sure as hell was feeling mighty ravenous.

Now, just in case you might be wondering about my brat, what with me and Lillian both right there in the old White Owl at the same damn time and I ain't said nothing about no snot-nosed kid running around all over the place a-hollering and raising hell, well, the kid was at home with Myrtle. Myrtle was Horace's wife, so we was paying Horace to cook in the

White Owl and Myrtle to watch the brat over at our house. We was sure supporting them two all right, but that was so I could go on about with my marshaling duties and Lillian could prance around the White Owl in her fancy dresses, not doing nothing worthwhile but just only spending my money on a goddamn business that was really a bust.

'Course, we sure wasn't hurting none for money. We had give old Bonnie Boodle a share of the Hooch House, but we still had our share in that thriving establishment, and me being the town marshal like I was, I still didn't allow no competition to be set up in Asininity to steal none of the Hooch House's business away from it. So if anyone around had a craving for a drink of whiskey or a glass of beer or for a woman's temporary feminine charms, and he didn't want to ride his ass all the way over to the county seat to satisfy any of them cravings, why, he just natural had to come into Harvey's Hooch House. That's the way I liked it, and that's the way I kept it. And then on top of all that I still had my pay from the town for being marshal. So we was doing all right, but like I think I done told you, we was really losing money on the White Owl.

Old Horace finally come dragging his ass out of the kitchen and brung me my steak dinner. I figured that old Lillian had made him do that 'cause she didn't want to be serving me her ownself. She was pissed off at me for coming into her posh establishment looking the way I was looking. She would have said that she was "put out." I never did understand that little saying of hers. I always felt more like I was the one being put out, you know, like put out with the dog or something like that. But I didn't care none. I tied into that steak right away, and old Horace, he could cook powerful good. I'll say that much for the old son of a bitch.

I was just about halfway through with my steak when old Happy come walking in, and he looked around, and then he seen me, and he come on over to the table where I was at. "Set your ass down," I said, still chawing on a bite of beef. "We'll get you a steak here in a minute." Then I yelled out over my shoulder. "Hey, Lillian."

"Barjack," Happy said, and just then I really looked up at him for the first time since I had woke up in the cell. I thought then that if Lillian had thought that I looked bad, just wait till she gets a look at old Happy. He was a hell of a mess, I mean to tell you. His shirt was tore, and it was dirty from him having rolled around on the floor. He had a mouse on his right eye, and there was dried blood caked in his hair, and it showed down the side of his face and neck and clear down onto his shirtfront. "Barjack," he said, "that prisoner over there needs a meal. I went ahead and untied his hands for him, but he ain't had nothing to eat since well before I brung him in to you."

"Son of a bitch won't die," I said. "We get finished here, I'll have something sent on over to him."

Lillian come on out then, and it tuck her a few seconds to recognize Happy, as messed up as he was. Then she said, "Happy! What in the world happened to you?" And she sounded so sweet and so concerned.

I was recalling the way she had acted when I come in just a few minutes before that.

"Aw, nothing much," he said, and I will say I was proud of him for that. "I just been out on the trail is all."

"Lillian," I said, "old Happy here needs him a steak and a drink."

"I think I need coffee," Happy said, "but I could go for that steak."

"We'll take care of you right away, Happy," Lillian said in her sweetest and most businesslike voice. Goddamn it, I thought, that damned voice tingled like bells. Hell, that was half of what had caught me in her snares in the first place, but then, she hardly ever give it that tone anymore when she was talking to just me. She went on back to the kitchen, and directly she come back and put a cup of coffee in front of Happy. "Sugar and cream?" she asked him. "Well, yes, ma'am," he said. "I'd like that."

She hustled her butt away and come back real quick with the stuff. Happy thanked her real nice, and she tittered over him a bit more. Final, she left us alone.

"Barjack," Happy said, "someone sure stomped me good. Was it you?"

"I don't know, Happy," I said. "If it was me, you stomped me back just as bad. Hell, boy, I hurt all over."

Pretty soon Lillian fetched out Happy's food and served him real sweet and made over him some more before she left us in peace again. Well, he tackled that food just as eager as I had done mine, and when he was close to done, I ordered up another one to go on back over to the jailhouse. I figured if I was to pay for three meals it would make Lillian's cash drawer for that day look better and maybe somehow improve her disposition whenever we both got back to the house that evening. Besides, I meant to write up a chit over at my office and turn it in to the town to get myself reimbursed. After all, it was business. I was taking care of a prisoner and the man what had brought the prisoner in.

While we was waiting for the prisoner's steak to get cooked, I poured myself another glass of whiskey. Lillian had just refilled Happy's coffee cup. "Well," I said, thinking to make it real official about the business meal, "who is the son of a bitch?"

Happy looked up at me. "Huh?" he said.

"That son of a bitch over in my jail," I said. "The one what's fixing to get the best steak for fifty miles around courtesy of the town of Asininity. Who the hell is he?"

"Oh," said Happy. "Well, he's old Jug Marlin, and he's wanted for murder." He went to digging in his pockets, and he come up with a folded-up paper, which he then laid out on the table and smoothed over. Then he turned it around so I could take me a good look at it. There was the picture, and it sure as hell was the same man I had in my jail, and it give the name of Jug Marlin, all right. It also said that there was a $500 reward for his capture.

"Looks like you got some money coming to you, Happy," I said.

He grinned. "Yeah," he said.

"I reckon," I said. "You know I'll have to wire Denver for it?"

He nodded. "Yeah," he said. "I remember the routine."

The reward was being offered out of the United States Marshal's Office in Denver, so in order to pay it to Happy, I'd have to send a wire to get the payment authorized. Once I got that, I could pay him out of the town's coffers and rest assured that the federal folks in Denver would give us our money back. "How'd you happen to get ahold of him, Happy?" I asked.

"Well, it was just kind of by accident," Happy said. "You know I wouldn't take on no gunfighter on purpose. Not even for no five hundred dollars."

"So how'd it happen?" I asked him again.

"It was down south of here," he said. "Down in that little old town of Drivel. You know?"

"I know the place," I said. "Go on."

"Well," he said, "I was just kind of looking around, you know, to see if there was any jobs available. Just anything. I'd do most anything 'cept work on a ranch. I can't handle cows. Well, I hadn't found me nothing. Didn't really expect to in that little old place, and I didn't even have no cash left on me to get myself a place to sleep. I was kind of thinking that I'd just ride all night long and just slip right on through Asininity in the dark, you know, 'cause—well, anyhow, I was figuring to ride on up to the county seat. Figured I'd have a better chance of finding some kind of employment up there."

"Get to the goddamned point, Happy," I said.

"How the hell did you get your hands on old Marlin there?"

"I had just stepped out of the saloon there, down in Drivel, you know," Happy said. "It's called the Yellow Dog, and just then I seen a for real yellow dog walk up onto the sidewalk a few feet down to my right. I was thinking how funny it was to come out of the Yellow Dog and then to see a yellow dog, and right then he puked right in the middle of the sidewalk. Right there. Hell, Barjack, it seemed almost deliberate."

I was beginning to get real impatient with old Happy's way of telling a tale, and I said, "Go on."

"Well, just about then this feller come walking down the sidewalk, coming from my left, you see," Happy said, "and he walked right past me with his nose stuck up in the air, you know, and he just kept on a-going, never give a nod nor said a howdy, and then he stepped right smack in the middle of that fresh pile of dog puke. Well, his foot slipped, a course, and he went a-flying, and he come down hard right on the back of his head. Knocked him cold. Hell, it kind of scared me. I thought maybe he'd been killed, you know, so I run right on over to him and picked up his head. I asked him if he was all right, but he never answered me none. He was for sure out cold.

"Then another feller come along. 'By God. How'd you do it?' he asked me. I said, 'Whut?' He said, 'How the hell did you get old Jug Marlin?' Well, then I recognized the name, and I just acted kind of cool like. I dropped old Marlin's head back down on the sidewalk, and I slipped his gun out of his holster and tucked it in my belt. Then I rolled him over on his face, and I asked that feller if he could fetch me a short piece of rope, and he did, and when he brung it back to me, he had a for-sure crowd around him.

"One of them was their town lawman, but he said that he couldn't accommodate the prisoner and didn't have no funds to pay me the reward, so I'd have to get him to a bigger town. I tied old Marlin's hands real good behind his back, found out where his horse was at and loaded him on it, and then I headed right for Asininity with him. I knew that you could get the reward for me. I guess that's about it."

I set there for a minute thinking. "Dog puke," I said.

Happy grinned. "Yeah," he said. "Dog puke. A yellow dog, too."

Lillian brought out Marlin's meal on a tray with a rag laid over it, and I paid her for all three meals and all my drinks. That did perk her up some. Happy give her a polite nod, and she thanked him real kindly. She never said nothing to me one way or the other, and I counted myself real lucky on that score, but I figgered it was only just because old Happy was there with me. "Come on," I said, and I picked up the tray. "Let's go get the paperwork done on old Marlin and send that there wire." Happy followed me out of the White Owl, and we walked on over to my office.

We went inside, and old Marlin popped right up off the cot immediate-like. He seen the tray, and his natural streak of cussedness overcome him right then. I reckon he had just about forgot what I'd said to him earlier about keeping his mouth shut. "Well, it's about

31

time," he said. I set it down on my desktop.

"Don't act smart," I said, "or I'll just eat it myself. I done et one, but I reckon I could handle another, and I'll set right here, and I'll eat the son of a bitch right here in front of your little slit eyes. You got anything more smart to say, smart-ass?"

"No, sir," he said.

"Go on and give it to him," I told Happy, and Happy did. Then I went and sniffed the air a bit. "Something in here smells like dog puke," I said.

"It's the seat of my britches," Marlin said. "And the bottom of my right boot."

"Take the damned things off," I said, and he did like I told him. Then I said to Happy, "Find a stick to get them things out of here."

I started in on the paperwork while Happy went outside, and Marlin started wolfing down his meal. Happy come back in right away with a long stick, and he poked it through the bars and lifted up Marlin's nasty britches. He tuck them to the back door and throwed them out. Then he come back and got the boot and done the same thing. I finished up the paperwork, and then I said to Happy, "Let's go send that wire," and me and him walked out, leaving Marlin eating in the cell alone without no britches on and with only one boot.

On the way to the telegraph office, I stepped into Matty's laundry. Matty wasn't there, but her husband Eli was. "Eli," I said, "out behind my office there's a boot and a pair of britches that's got dog puke on them. Pick them up and clean them up and deliver them back over to my office along with the bill. The town'll pay you."

Me and old Happy went on down to the telegraph office, and I give little Herman Simpson the note what I wanted him to send over the wire, and I told him to send the bill to my office. "Soon as you get an answer on that," I said, "bring it to me down at the Hooch House." He promised he would, and me and Happy walked out and down the sidewalk back to Harvey's. Well, it was afternoon by then, and so the place had a few customers. Most of them knowed Happy, and they swarmed all over him saying howdy and asking him stuff like where he'd been and how long he meant to be in town.

I walked over to the bar and got a bottle and two glasses. Bonnie was there, leaning her elbows on the bar and looking out at the small crowd. "Get your glass and set with us," I said. She got her glass and her own bottle. She never liked my own brand. Then she followed me to a table and set down. We poured ourselves each a drink, and I held my glass up toward her. "Here's to the good old times," I said. She raised up her glass and clicked it against mine. "I'll drink to that," she said.

"Bonnie," I said, lowering my voice somewhat, "will you tell me the truth before old Happy gets over here? Did you really screw old Happy way while ago?"

"Sure I did," she said. "You didn't think I'd do it, did you? Well, by God, I did."

"How was he?" I asked.

33

"He was pretty good, Barjack," she said, "but you know what?"

"What?" I said, and then she looked over at Happy and then leaned across the table to get close to me. I leaned over toward her, and then she said in a real low voice, "I think it was his first time."

I think my eyes opened real wide at that, and I said, "Really?"

"Really," she said, "but don't you dare say nothing to Happy. I wouldn't want him to know I told you that."

"Hell," I said, "I wouldn't say nothing to a man about a thing like that."

We each leaned back in our chairs and took a drink. Then, "Barjack," she said, "he was pretty good, but he wasn't the best I ever had."

"No?" I said.

"No," she said. "You want to know who was the best?"

"All right," I said. "Who was the best, Bonnie?"

"You was, Barjack," she said. "You was always the best."

Well, that puffed me up some. 'Course, I was always pretty sure that would be the case, but it was nice to hear her say it out loud. I grinned, and I said, "Well, thank you for that, old girl. You know, I could say the same thing for you."

Well, I'll be damned if she didn't actual kind of blush and then look real soft, which wasn't easy for Bonnie Boodle, and she said, "Really, Barjack? Do you mean that? Was I the best you ever had?"

"The best, Bonnie," I said, and I tuck me another

34

drink. Then her soft look vanished, and she tuck on her hard and mean look.

"And you had to go and throw it all away on account of—"

Just then old Happy come walking over to set with us, having broke loose from all them well-wishing folks, and I remember thinking that Happy's timing had never been so good before in his whole entire life. I poured him a drink and shoved it at him. "There you go, partner," I said. "Say, you remember old Bonnie Boodle here, don't you?"

Chapter Three

Me and old Happy and old Bonnie Boodle was just a-setting there and drinking and reminiscing about the good old times, and after a while here come that little old Simp, and he was a waving a wire message at me. "Here it is, Barjack," he hollered. "It came. Here's the answer to that message you sent to Denver." Soon as he was close enough to me, I jerked the son of a bitch right out of his little soft white hand.

"Simp," I said, "you sure as hell got yourself named right. What if I was to have a need to keep my messages to myself? Huh? What if it was some kind of important secret I was a-waiting for, and then you went around yelling it all over the whole damn town? What about that?"

Simp kind of hung his head a little bit. "Is it a secret, Barjack?" he said.

"Well, it ain't now, is it?" I said.

"I reckon not," he said.

"Aw," I said, "get on out of here before I decide to throw your ass in jail."

He got out all right, in a hurry, and Happy looked at me real serious-like. "Is that there a secret message, Barjack?" he said. "Me and Bonnie can leave you alone to read it if you want us to."

He had done lifted his ass up out of the chair. "Sit down," I said. "Hell, it's been so long since I seen you that I just about forgot that you're might' near as dumb as old Simp. It's about your prisoner. That's all."

"Oh," he said. "What's it say?"

"Well, let's see here now," I said, studying on the paper. "First thing it says here is that you damn well get the reward. Old Marlin, he's worth five hundred, all right. I can pay you out of the town coffers okay, and then the United States Marshal's Office out of Denver will send it on back to the town. That's in case you can't afford to lay around here long enough for it to get here from Denver, or if you can't go on over there after it yourself. That's how come they do it that way."

"So I'll get paid?" Happy said.

"That's just what I said, ain't it? Ain't that what I said?" I do sometimes get tired all to hell with the dumb asses around me. "Now, wait a minute," I said. "There's something else here."

"What?" said Happy.

"What is it?" Bonnie asked.

"It says here that I'm requested to deliver the pris-

37

oner into the hands of the U.S. marshal in Denver," I told them. "Personal."

"Does the marshal have to have him in Denver before he'll send my money?" Happy asked.

"Damn it, Happy," I said, "how many times I got to tell you a thing before it soaks into your goddamned thick skull? What you got in there for brains, anyhow? Dog puke? That's what it is. Yellow dog puke. Come on. Let's go see old Peester. I'll get your goddamned money for you right now."

It wasn't really that I was so damned anxious to take care of old Happy, but the thought of the trip to Denver had got me real itchy right quick. I wasn't none too crazy about Denver neither. It wasn't that. Not a damn bit. What it really was was that I seen it right away as a chance of getting my ass away from Lillian and that damned kid for a while. Maybe a good long while. I couldn't hardly stand to just set there in the Hooch House with a prospect like that staring me right smack in the eyeballs.

So I just popped right up out of my chair, and old Happy, he done the same thing, and then he followed me out to the street. We walked along on over to Peester's rebuilt office. It was still right there where it had been whenever it had got blowed away during that Benson frolic. I barged right on in the way I always do whenever I have a need to see the old shyster son of a bitch. "Peester," I said, and he looked up at me from behind his big desk on which he had been writing on some papers, lawyering work, I guessed. "You remember old Happy Bonapart, I reckon," I said.

"Hmm?" he muttered. "Oh. Oh, yes indeed. How are you, Bonapart? It's been a while now, hasn't it?"

"Yes, sir," Happy said.

"Now, I didn't come in here just to have a god-damned reunion," I said. "Take a look at this here," and I laid that wire on his desk under his nose. He must have read it through two or three times, as long as it tuck for him to look back up and say something.

"You have this Marlin in our jail?" he asked me.

"That's right," I said, thinking what a dumb question that was, him having just read the damned wire message. "Old Happy here brung him in this morning. Captured the son of a bitch all by his lonesome down in Drivel and brung him up here. So you need to sign a chit I can take over to the bank to get Happy his reward money. And then you need to sign another one for expense money for me to deliver the son of a bitch to Denver. I'll need enough for two stage tickets and for meals all along the way. I'll need some for a hotel room in Denver, too, and for one ticket on back home."

The pettifogging, skinflint old bastard acted for all hell like the money was coming right straight out of his own personal bank account, but he did sign the goddamned chits. He didn't have no choice. I poked them into my pocket. He looked at me, and I was just a standing there. "Is there something else?" he asked me.

"Yeah," I said. "I'm going to be gone for a spell, and you'll need someone to be minding the marhal's office. Besides all that, I been without a deputy for a time now, ever since the Bensons blowed the town up." Actual, it had been me that had blowed up the town that time, but I thought it was for the best to lay it all off on the Bensons. "I want you to put old Happy here back on the payroll. He's had experience in the job before, as you well know. Besides, him collecting that there reward money, he won't need no advance in pay to help him get settled in."

That last eased old Peester's tightwad brain just a little bit.

"Barjack," Happy said as we was walking together toward the bank, "I never asked you for no job."

"I know that," I said.

"And you never asked me if I wanted one," he said, "so I never told you if I did or I didn't."

"You told me you was looking for a job," I said.

"Well," he said, "yeah. I did tell you that."

"Then quit your damn bitching," I said. "You got one now. And you ain't even going to have the boss around to worry about. Not for a while. Hell, you'll be on your own. You'll be in charge." Dragging old Happy along with me, I tuck us into the bank, and we come out of there with our pockets full of the town's money. Then I went by the stage office and got me two tickets to Denver, one for me and one for old Jug Marlin. I could have wished for better company on that long trip than old Jug, but then, I'd get rid of him in Denver, and then I'd be all alone by myself in Denver a hell of a long ways from home and Lillian and the kid. I figured I'd have myself a damn good time, then head slowly on back. It crossed my mind once or twice that I could just stay the hell away, I mean for good, but then, I sure did have a sweet setup there in Asininity. It would take a hell of a lot of time to build up anything like that somewheres else, and I wasn't getting no younger.

Well, the damned stage would be arriving in Asininity around noon the next day, and it would take off for points west shortly after that, so I had the whole entire rest of the day and night and the next morning even to fill up with something to try to keep the hours from just dragging on. I was damned anxious to get that trip started, I can tell you. Old Happy, he wanted to go on and find hisself a place to live and get settled on in, so I braced myself and went on home to get my valise and pack some clothes in it. Soon as I opened the door to my little house, a goddamned baseball hit me smack in the center of the forehead, and the little bastard commenced to laughing like hell.

Well, I got my goddamned valise and throwed some clothes in it and got the hell out of there as fast as I could manage it, with the kid hollering at me and pestering me, and Myrtle apologizing all to hell all the way. When I final stepped out of there and slammed that front door behind myself, I stood for a second or two breathing a deep sigh of relief. Then I hustled on back down to my office. I stuck several boxes of shells into my valise. I didn't expect no trouble delivering the damn prisoner, but you never know. I was all packed, had my cash and my tickets, so I figured I'd best go tell Lillian what I was up to and get that miserable chore out of the way. I left my valise in the office and walked back over to the White

Owl Supper Club. At the front door, I stood up as tall as I could and tuck myself a deep breath. Then I opened the door and walked on in.

Lillian had a few customers in the place, and she was kind of busy hustling around and playing hostess to them all. She acted like she didn't even see me come in, so I just went around behind the damned bar and poured myself some whiskey. I was on my third glass whenever she bothered to slow down just a little within a few feet of where I was setting. "Be sure you pay for those drinks," she said. She started to walk on away from me, but I jumped up and grabbed her by an arm. "Wait up," I said. "I got to talk to you a minute." She said, "It had better be important. Can't you see I'm busy here?" She let me put her down in a chair, and then I set down across the table from her. "I'm going on a trip, Lil," I said. I waited for some kind of an explosion, but it never come.

"Where are you going?" she asked me.

I answered her with another question. I said, "You recall that old Happy come in here with a prisoner?" She admitted that she did recollect such a thing, and then I told her about the wanted poster and the reward and the wire to Denver and the one back to me. "So I got to deliver the prisoner to Denver," I concluded, and I do believe that she seemed almost to take some pleasure from that news. "Anyhow," I said, "things will be all right here, 'cause Happy's done got back his deputy badge, and he'll be in charge of the marshaling business here while I'm gone."

"All right," she said. "Will you be leaving on to-morrow's stage?"

"That's right," I said, "and I won't be home to-night, neither. I got to stay in the office and watch that there prisoner. I ain't got no choice in the matter. I didn't hardly think that I could stick old Happy with that chore right off. Matter of fact, I let him take off and see if he can get hisself settled in somewhere."

"Well," she said, standing up and looking around the room, "I guess I'll see you when you get back." And then she pasted on her professional smile and hustled over to one of the tables to check on her customers there. I was glad that she hadn't made no scene. I sure didn't want her yelling and screaming at me none, but to tell you the God's truth, I was just a mite disappointed that she didn't seem to give a damn whether she ever seen me again or not. I reckoned I was going to have to think about that some. I finished off my drink and left the place, and I walked straight on over to the Hooch House.

Inside I found old Happy a-setting beside Bonnie at a table close to the bar. I didn't think nothing of it at the time, but instead I walked over to the bar and told Aubrey to fetch me up a tumbler and a bottle, and he did. I tuck them over to the table and set myself down beside Bonnie.

"Hello, Barjack," she said. "Happy says you're going to Denver tomorrow."

I said, "That's right, and what's more, I done said bye-bye to Lillian. I'm sleeping in the jailhouse to-night." I poured myself a glass full and tuck a gulp.

"You'll be coming back, won't you?" she asked me. I looked up at her, and then I glanced on over at Happy. He didn't look at me, just down at his glass there on the table in front of him. Right then I read something in their faces what I wasn't sure what it was, but it made me kind of pissed off at them both.

"Why the hell wouldn't I be coming back?" I said. "I got my job here and my business interests, not to mention my wife and kid. All I'm doing is just a part of my job. That's all. You seen that there wire, Happy. Tell her about it."

"It just said that I was to get my reward," Happy said, "and that you was to deliver the prisoner to Denver to the U.S. marshal there."

I shot a hard look at Bonnie. "See?" I said.

"I didn't mean nothing by it," she said. "I was just asking. That's all. I'll miss you while you're gone."

"I bet you'll just be counting the days till I get back," I said, and I sure as hell to this day don't know how come I was feeling so hostile toward Bonnie and Happy just then, but I guess that it had something to do with the way old Lillian had behaved when I told her about the trip. I believe that my brain was working up to tell me that there really wasn't no one that give a damn about me, and they was all hoping—Lillian and the brat, Happy and Bonnie—they was all hoping that they'd never see me again.

Now, I mean to tell you that for a man what's used to feeling his own importance such as I was then, that's a somewhat uneasy sensation to have—the sudden coming on you of the sense that if you was to just up and walk right off the edge of the world there wouldn't be no one who would even worry about it or give a damn. I mean, a man likes to think that he'll be missed by someone. If I was laid out in a pine box and dumped down in a hole, I was thinking, would Lillian be up there weeping as they throwed dirt in on top of me? Hell. Not likely. And would Happy and Bonnie even be standing there by the grave? I didn't think so. I felt like hitting Happy again, but I knowed that I didn't really have no excuse, so I just set still and tuck another gulp of whiskey, and what it done was it made me feel sadder and at the same time meaner. I felt like some kind of a tussle, all right.

"Bonnie, old girl," I said, "let's you and me go upstairs for a little romp."

"Barjack," she said, and the tone of her voice was like she was admonishing me, you know.

"Well?" I said.

"Not just now, Barjack," she said. "I'm setting here visiting with Happy. Just set with us awhile. Okay? Happy ain't yet told us what all he's been doing while he was away."

"Hell," I said, "I done asked him, and all he said was 'This and that.' He ain't got nothing more to tell. Come on, now. Let's go on up. Goddamn it, Bonnie, I'm leaving tomorrow, and I'm like to be gone for quite a spell."

Then I seen her give a look to old Happy, and that little son of a bitch kind of give a quick nod back to her like as if he was saying to her, go on, it's all right, and that really pissed me off. Bonnie started to get up. "Come on, Barjack," she said, and then I said, "Hell. I done lost interest." She set back down then.

"Barjack," she said, "what's got you in such a foul mood? How come you're sleeping tonight in the jail-house, anyway? Is it Lillian?"

When she said that, I wasn't so sure no more. It come to me just then that I was mad at Lillian, and here I was taking it all out on my only two real friends. I tuck myself another drink, draining my glass, and then I poured it full again. "Aw, just forget it," I said. You see, I was of a sudden all kind of fuddled up in the brain. I didn't know no longer just who the hell I was mad at or why I was pissed off at them, either. I lifted up my glass high and said, "Here's to goddamn Denver. I sure as hell hope they've got plenty of good whiskey there, 'cause I mean to drink up my share of it."

The next thing I recall, I was waking up on a cot in one of my own damn jail cells. I set up real slow and easy, and then I heard that bastard Marlin say, "Good mornin' to you, Sheriff." I kind of moaned, and I said, "I ain't no goddamned sheriff, you simple fool. I'm town marshal of this here town, and you and me is fixing to make us a long trip together to Denver commencing about noontime. I reckon they mean to hang you out there. I ain't decided yet if I'll stick around and watch it."

I got myself up kind of slow-like and walked real easy out into my office. I looked over at the clock, and it was just about eight in the morning. I could see through the window that folks was moving around out on the sidewalks already. I found my hat and put it on my head and went to the door. "Hey," Marlin hollered, "do I get any breakfast in here?" He pissed me off. "I'll think about it," I said, and I went on out. I was thinking about whiskey, but when Marlin said breakfast, that put me in mind of it, so I walked down to the end of the street to a little joint called Maudie's. The Hooch House nor the White Owl, neither one never fixed no breakfast. It come too early in the day. I found Happy in there wolfing down a mess of greasy taters. I went over and set with him.

"Good morning, Barjack," he said.

"Goddamn it, Happy," I said, "it's after eight. Why ain't you at work yet?"

"You never give me no key to the office, Barjack," he said. Well, hell, I couldn't argue with that, so I just ordered me up some ham and eggs and stuff and started in slurping on some hot coffee. I dug a key out of my pocket and slapped it on the table. "So," I said, "where'd you sleep last night?" Old Happy turned real red in the face, and just as soon as he done that I figgered I knowed all right where the little son of a bitch had slept the night. The back-stabbing bastard had slept with Bonnie. That's what. I kind of bristled up some, but I controlled myself. Just then old Maudie brought along my plate, and neither me nor Happy said nothing till she had left again.

"Bonnie rented me a room upstairs in the Hooch House," Happy said.

"Oh," I said, "she did that, did she? That was real nice of her. Just right down the hall from her room, is it?"

"Hell, Barjack," he said, "all the rooms in the Hooch House is up and down one hallway."

"Hell," I said, "I know that."

I was thinking how one time I practical lived up there in Bonnie's room, but then that was before Lillian showed up in town, and it was me alone what

47

went out full tilt at Lillian and dumped old Bonnie, and that was why Bonnie like to have killed me. I guess it wasn't none of my business who Bonnie was putting out to, but still, all that logical kind of thinking didn't have nothing to do with what I was feeling just then.

"Barjack?" Happy said.

"What?" I said, not looking up at him but just continuing to wrassle with the ham and eggs on my plate.

"That stage'll be in at noon," he said.

"Hell," I said, "I know that."

"Don't you think that maybe you'd ought to take yourself a bath and change your clothes?" he said. "You're going for a long ride."

"You sound like Lillian," I said. "You filling in for her since she ain't here?"

"You still got blood on your shirt and coat," he said. "Some there on the side of your head. You're kind of dirty from rolling in the floor, and—"

"Ah, shut up," I said. "Go on over to the Hooch House and have them draw me a bath. Then get your ass on over to the office. You're on duty, you know."

Chapter Four

For once by God the damn stage was on time. I had gone ahead and cleaned myself up some and put on a fresh suit for the trip. Me and Happy, working together, had got old Marlin out of the cell and put some handcuffs on him. He had his britches and his boot back by then. I had latched one wrist, then run the other cuff and the chain down through his belt, and then latched the other wrist. That way his hands was cuffed together and sort of hooked to his waist. He looked kind of like he was playing with his own self, but he wouldn't be able to do much resisting that way. I shoved him on down to the station to wait for boarding-up time, and Happy and Bonnie showed up to see us off. I didn't see no sign of Lillian, though, nor the brat neither.

"What the hell are you two doing here?" I said.

"We just come to see you off," Bonnie said.

"There ain't no need for that," I said. "We all know I'm going. I'll see you when I get back, that's all. So long."

They looked at each other kind of funny. Then Happy give a kind of a shrug, and they walked on off. "You keep your damn eyes open," I yelled at Happy's back, "and take care of things around here while I'm gone. I don't want to come home to no mess. You hear me?"

"Your absence could wind up being permanent," Marlin said through a sneer.

I give him a hard look. "And you might not never make it all the way to Denver alive in order to get yourself hanged," I said. I shoved him backward and he fell down, setting in a chair. "Keep your goddamn mouth shut," I added for good measure. Just then old Preacher Harp come walking into the station, and he went up to the counter and bought hisself a ticket. "You going somewheres, Preacher?" I asked him.

"That should be obvious," he said in that arrogant tone of his.

"Going to be gone long?" I asked.

"I'm leaving this wretched town for good," he said.

"How come?" I said. "It's a peaceful town enough, ain't it?"

"It's a godless town, Marshal," he said. "I've fought the Devil here as long as I can. I'm worn out with the futile attempt. There's no need for a shepherd in a place where there's no flock to be tended."

"What the hell does that mean?" I asked him, scratching my head.

50

"Were you in church last Sunday?" he asked me, giving me a stern look.

"Well, no," I said. "I can't say that I was."

"Neither was anyone else," he said. "I'm weary with preaching to the wind. I'm abandoning this wretched place to the Devil. Let him rejoice in it. He'll have all your souls in hell in good time anyhow, and all of you will roast on spits and howl for all eternity. I rejoice in the thought."

"Well, I don't know nothing about that," I said, "and what's more, I don't give a damn." I glanced back over at my prisoner to make sure he was setting still, and he was. Then I felt the need for a drink, so I pulled the flask out of my pocket and tuck a slug from it. I had three full bottles of good stuff tucked into my valise, but I figured that it would either get tossed on top or stashed away in the damn boot, so I had fixed me up that flask in order to take care of emergencies along the way.

As I tucked the flask back in my pocket, I looked over at old sharp-nosed Harp just standing there so smug and self-righteous-like, and I said out loud, "God bless the man that invented whiskey."

"That's blasphemy, Marshal," he said. "You'd do well to think on eternity and the state of your sorry immortal soul."

"And you'd do well to take yourself a little drink now and then," I told him. "It might relax your stiff ass somewhat and wipe that sour-milk look off a your long face."

Well, old Howie come out from behind the counter then and walked outside. In another minute he come back in and told us to get our ass on the stage. It was ready to go. I picked up my valise and then grabbed hold of Marlin and hauled him up to his feet. I shoved him toward the door. The preacher heaved himself up and sniffed a long sniff through his nostrils. We all went outside, and old Goose Neck Adams, the driver, tuck my valise and put it in the boot. That was the only bag I seen, and I wondered how come the preacher didn't have none. Then Goose Neck strapped the boot down real good. I glanced up and seen that old Ash Face Morgan was riding shotgun.

Ash Face got his name because of his whiskers. No one ever seen him fresh shaved, but then his beard never did seem to grow neither. It seemed as how his whiskers had growed out just enough to make the bottom half of his face look like it had been rubbed over with ashes, and then it just stopped growing right there. Anyhow, he was billy hell with that shotgun, and I was glad enough to see him up there. Couple of years before, Sluefoot Gordon had stepped out in the middle of the road with a six-gun in each hand to stop the stage, and old Ash Face had blowed the head clean off Sluefoot's shoulders with his shotgun. I tuck some comfort in his presence, I can tell you.

Goose Neck opened up the door, and I shoved Marlin through it. As he was climbing up, I swatted his ass with the butt end of my Winchester. "Get in there," I said. I climbed in behind him and set myself down right across from him, and Preacher Harp followed me. He set beside Marlin, figgering, I guess, that I was a worse contamination than that murdering bastard. I did my best to find a comfortable way to set, having two Colts strapped on and a flask in my ass pocket and holding a Winchester in my hand. It was going to be a long ride—seven days, they said. It tuck me a while, but I final got my butt placed proper, and I leaned my rifle against the seat just by my left arm. I seen Marlin eyeball it.

"Marlin, you damn fool," I said, and I seen Harp wince just as if I'd gouged him in the ribs, "I seen you looking at that there Winchester. Look all you want, but if you try anything, I'll goddamn sure cheat the hangman. I can turn you in dead just as well as alive. You best try to keep that thought in your sorry-ass head."

Just then I heard some hollering out on the street. "Hold it up. Hold up the stage," someone was calling. "Wait for me." I looked out the window and seen Loren Van Pelt a-coming lickety-split and lugging two bags.

"We got a schedule," Goose Neck grumbled from up on the box.

"I have my ticket already," Van Pelt said. "All right, hell," said Goose Neck. "Toss your bags up and hand me up the ticket."

Van Pelt stuck the smaller of the two bags between his feet and heaved the other one up on top. Then he reached up to hand his ticket to Goose Neck. He picked up the smaller bag and said, "I'll hang on to this one."

Goose Neck said, "Suit yourself, but get on in there. We got to get going."

Van Pelt got in and set on the seat beside me. He looked kind of nervous, maybe because of my prisoner and all my guns, I thought at the time.

"Pelty," I said, "what the hell are you doing? Taking a vacation?" He pulled a hanky out of his pocket and kind of dabbed at his forehead.

"I wish I was," he said. "Mr. Markham is sending me to Denver on bank business. Whew. If I'd have missed this stage, he'd have fired me for sure." Just then old Goose Neck hollered and flicked them long-ass reins, and them six fine, high-stepping horses tuck off fast. The coach give a hell of a lurch, and old Marlin come flying right over on top of me. I shoved him hard back over onto his seat and hauled out my right-hand Colt, thumbing back the hammer at the same time. I aimed the thing right at his nose.

"Try anything like that again, you son of a bitch," I said, "and I'll blow your brains out."

"I didn't try nothing, Barjack," he said. "I swear it. The damn coach just throwed me. That's all. Hell, the way you got me trussed up here, I can't hold on to nothing."

I felt sort of foolish, 'cause whenever he said that, I could tell that it was for real what had happened. I eased the hammer down on my Colt and poked it back into its holster. "Stretch your damn legs out and prop your feet against the bottom of this seat here," I said. The coach rocked and rolled on down the road, and I could damn well tell that it was going to be a hell of a long ride. I asked myself why in hell I hadn't made old Happy take Marlin to Denver, and then I thought again about Lillian and the brat, and I decided that I had likely made the right decision. I'd just have to suffer the miseries of the road in exchange for the other miseries at home, that's all.

Well, the ride up north to the county seat didn't take too much time, but my ass was already dead when we got there. I was sure glad to get out and stretch my legs. Goose Neck told us not to go far unless we wanted to be left behind. We was only going to be there for a few minutes. There was men, women, and kids all around on the street. There always was when a stagecoach come into town. And I thought I seen a face in the crowd catch the eye of old Jug Marlin, but then they each looked off in other directions, and I kind of forgot about it. Then I seen that they was fixing to load up a couple of more passengers, and I didn't want to lose my place nor Marlin's, so I made him get back in, and then I did too.

I watched out the window, and I seen Goose Neck toss some more bags up on top, and I settled myself in as good as I could. "Brace your goddamned feet," I said to Marlin, and he did. Van Pelt and Harp clumb back in then and set again where they had been before, and then Goose Neck opened the door across from me and helped an old woman in. She settled her broad ass down beside the preacher, and then in come another one, but this one was a young thing. There was no place for her to set but beside old Pelty. Being surrounded now, Pelty pulled his little bag up close to his chest and hugged it tight with both arms. The smell of perfume filled up the coach and damn near overwhelmed me. I wished that Goose Neck would get us to rolling, 'cause being what you might call a real man's man, I sure didn't want to swoon right there in front of everyone. Not to mention that me swooning away would give a good chance of breaking out to old Marlin, you know.

I noticed then that Marlin was kind of ogling that young woman, and I was about to say something to him when Goose Neck got us going with another lurch. Pretty soon enough wind and dust was blowing in on us that it saved me from that contemplated horrible embarassment that I was afraid might happen to me. I like a little sweet smell on a woman as much as any man, but I sure as hell hate to be cooped up close with an overabundance of the stuff, and one or both of them two women was damn sure over-abundant.

I had got me such a close call that I decided that I just had to have me a little snort, so I pulled my flask out and tuck me a drink. Damn, it felt good. I put the cap back on and shoved the flask back in my pocket.

"Hey, Barjack," Marlin said. "I could sure use a little taste of that there stuff." I seen Harp a-frowning at me.

"I didn't fetch that along to waste on the likes of you," I said to Marlin. Harp said, "A man who pours the Devil into his mouth and down his filthy gullet washeth his own soul straight to hell."

"You didn't get that out of no goddamned Bible, Preacher," I said. "You just made it up right out of your own head."

"Marshal," Harp said, "if you have no respect for a man of the cloth, at least show some common courtesy for ladies."

"I have the utmost respect for ladies," I said. "If I

didn't have, you would likely have heard some real cussing out of my filthy mouth. You mind your business, Preacher, and I'll mind mine."

Old Harp looked away from me and plucked the hat off his head. He looked at the old woman, then at the young one, and I thought I seen some lechery in his look then. "I'm the Reverend Pick Harp, ladies," he said. "At your service."

"How nice to have you along, Reverend," said the old gal. "It's a comfort." The preacher smiled a sour smile and thanked the old gal.

The young one almost giggled, and she put her hand in front of her mouth, and she said, "Pardon me, Reverend, I don't mean to make fun, but 'Pick Harp', well, it does have a—well—almost comical ring to it, doesn't it? Pick Harp?"

"It's a cross I must bear humbly and with patience, miss," he said. "Oh, pardon me. Is it miss?"

"Yes, Reverend," she said. "Miss Emma Purdy, and this is my aunt, Idabelle Purdy. We're traveling to Denver together."

"It's a great pleasure, ladies," old Harp said. "As I was saying about the name, it's a cross I must bear. My good parents, rest their souls, being ardent southern sympathizers, named me after that indomitable old warrior, Pickett. I don't know if they ever considered the . . . ring of the name."

"Oh, I think it's a fine name, Reverend," said Miss Emma Purdy. She kind of glanced around at the rest of us, and Harp harrumphed.

"Mr. Van Pelt there," he said, "works at the bank

in Asininity. Mr. Barjack is the town marshal, and—that—is his prisoner."

At them words, Marlin nodded his head. He couldn't tip his hat, 'cause his hands was locked to his belt. "How do, ladies," he said. "It's surely a pleasure to have such nice company along on this here trip to my uncertain future."

"You keep your yap shut," I said, and I give him a swift kick in the leg with the sharp toe of my boot.

"Ow," he hollered. "That hurt, Barjack."

"Marshal," the preacher snapped at me, "that was entirely uncalled for. The man is a prisoner in your charge. He should be treated humanely, not like some animal. You are responsible for his well-being."

"That's just what the hell he is," I said. "He's a cold-blooded, murdering animal, and I just thought that these here ladies didn't need the likes of him talking to them. I feel like my main responsibility is the safety and well-being of the innocent citizens around me. That's all."

"From what I've heard so far on this trip," Harp said, "your language has been much more offensive than his."

"Yes, Mr. Barjack," the young Purdy said. "I mean, Mr.—your prisoner—did us no harm. Really."

"Well, pardon me all to hell," I said. "Mr. Jug Marlin, may I kindly introduce you real good and proper to these here fine Purdy ladies? I'd loose your hands for you so you could take hold of each of theirs real genteel-like, but only I don't want to take a chance on you getting hold of none of my guns and blowing any of our livers out, so you'll just have to nod your head and say howdy."

Well, old Marlin, he nodded his head again, once at each lady, but he didn't say nothing. I reckon he was afraid that I'd kick him again, or something worse. The two ladies just looked straight ahead and lifted their noses. Old Harp, though, he looked right at Marlin and he had a real brotherly look of love on his face and he said, "Brother, God loves all his children. Have you repented of your wrongdoing and your evil ways?"

Marlin give me a timid look, and I just shrugged.

"Yes, sir, your reverendness," Marlin said. "I most surely have. I done some wicked things in my time, and I'm genuine sorry for all of them."

"God will forgive you, my son," Harp said.

"You just called him brother," I said. "If he's your brother and your son, you must have slept with your own mother."

Well, I reckon I really shouldn't ought to have said that, but I did. I don't know why, but I was in a sour mood already when I left Asininity, 'cause of Lillian and Bonnie and old Happy, and then, too, I never did like that hypocritical bastard of a preacher neither. Them two ladies had tuck up with him right off, and that pissed me off, and then that wimpy little bastard Pelty, well, he didn't hardly count none at all. So I just natural said what come into my mind, and a course, if you think logical, I was right about what I said anyhow. But that didn't seem to make no difference.

Both ladies squealed real loud-like as if they was

awful horrified, and the preacher straightened up stiff as a board and shouted out, "Barjack!" Old Ash Face leaned down over the side of the coach trying to look in the window. "What's wrong in there?" he hollered.

"Stop this coach at once," shouted Harp.

Well, pretty soon old Goose Neck had hauled in the team, and him and Ash Face had crawled down off the box. Goose Neck especial looked right agitated.

"What the hell's going on?" he said.

"Ain't no problems here," I said.

"I demand that Barjack be put out of the coach," Harp said.

"How come?" Goose Neck asked him.

"He insists on using the most foul language imaginable in front of two ladies, a gentleman, and a man of the cloth," Harp said. "I believe that the company owes us the comfort of a ride free from that kind of abuse. We have all paid our fares—"

"And I have, too," I said. "Mine and Marlin's. You can't have us put off of nothing, with all your pious crap."

"You see?" said Harp. "You see?" And he was fair dancing with agitation.

"Barjack," said Goose Neck, "have you for real been talking that way in front of these folks?"

"I got tired of listening to this preacher prattle," I said, "and I reckon I got as many rights as he does. He called old Marlin here his brother, and then he called him son. All I done was point out that if he was Marlin's father and his brother, he must have slept with his own mother. You tell me if you can see

60

any other way that could a happened? If you do, I'll take back my words and eat them."

"Preacher," said Goose Neck, "it seems to me that Barjack's right on that point. But, Barjack, I don't want you working up my other passengers no more. Right or wrong, don't get them riled. I don't want no more unscheduled stops like this, and you all shouldn't, either, if you ever want to get where you're going. Now, ever'one get back inside and try to keep things quiet."

"I demand that Barjack be put out," Harp said, and I seen purple veins a-standing out on his forehead and his neck.

"I ain't got no room on top," Goose Neck said, "and besides, it's against company regulations to put passengers up on top. And I sure as hell ain't leaving no one out here in the middle of nowhere. Your demands don't mean nothing. Get back inside now, all of you, 'cause I'm moving on."

Goose Neck didn't even bother looking back to make sure we was all reloaded. He clumb up on the box and snapped them reins. Old Harp just got the door closed on time. I felt kind of smug, but I decided not to rub it in. I give Marlin a look, and then I settled back, pulled my hat down over my eyes, and made out to get some shut-eye.

I know that I really did drop off for a bit, 'cause a sudden jar of the coach brought me back wide awake all at once. I give a quick look at Marlin, and he was sure giving me a hard look, but I guess he hadn't dared to try nothing. I checked my guns, being real casual about it, and ever'thing was all right. I won-

Robert J. Conley

dered what time it was getting to be, but I didn't want
to ask none of them stiffs in the coach with me. Looking out the window, I seen that the sun was getting
low, and I did feel a gnawing in my guts telling me
that I was some hungry. No one was talking. I reckoned that they had talked themselves out.

I hauled out my flask, and I seen Marlin lick his
lips and the preacher scowl. I tuck off its lid and had
me a long drink. It tasted good, and it did relieve that
gut gnawing, at least for a while. I lidded it again and
put it away. The preacher was still giving me a hard
look, and I said, "Pick Harp, you just as well set your
stare somewheres else. The Devil's done got his claws
dug in me real deep, and he ain't likely to let loose.
Not for the likes of you."

Just then old Ash Face yelled down from his perch
up on the box. "Stop ahead," he called out.

Chapter Five

The coach made a sudden hard turn to the right in order to pull into the way station, and the lurch of it throwed old Pelty right up against me and Miss Purdy, leaning all over him. He clutched that little bag of his tighter than ever. On the other seat the same thing happened. The old lady laid on Harp, and Harp squashed against Marlin. The ladies squealed a bit, and the coach come right again. Pretty soon old Goose Neck hauled them in, and we stopped and set there rocking a bit. Goose Neck had clumb down, and he opened the door on the other side and helped the ladies out. I popped open the door on my side and got on down, toting along my Winchester. Goddamn but I was stiff and sore. I pulled out my handy flask for a little relaxer.

"Hey," Marlin said, "what about me?"

"Come on out," I said.

"I can't grab hold of the door or nothing," he said. "I need some help."

"All right," I said, tucking my flask away secure. "I'll give you a hand." I reached up and tuck hold of his shirtfront and jerked him out the door. He tried to get his feet under him, but it didn't work, and he landed flat on his belly. "Oh," I said. "You all right?" He coughed and spluttered and spit some dirt out of his mouth. Then he sneaked his knees up under him. He looked pretty funny like that, what with his hands hooked up the way they was to his belt.

"Barjack, you piece of dog—," he said.

"You're the one what slides in dog puke," I said, "and watch the way you talk to me." Then I give him a quick kick in the ass and plowed his nose in the dirt again.

"Supper's on inside," Ash Face said. Goose Neck and the agent was busy changing the team, and I tuck hold of Marlin by his collar and pulled him to his feet.

"Come on," I said, shoving him toward the little building. Harp was escorting the ladies in that direction, and Pelty was hustling along behind them, still clutching that bag up tight against his chest.

"Barjack," Marlin said, "unhook me. I need to go to the outhouse."

I shoved him around to the backside of the building close to the outdoor john, and I unlocked one wrist. "Hurry it up," I said, "or there won't be no food left for us."

Marlin pulled the chain and the one cuff on through

64

his belt and run into the john. I stood there a-waiting for him, and I pulled out my flask for another swig. It burned me all the way down my gullet, but it was a good smooth burning, so I tuck another. I waited a bit longer, and then I hollered out, "Hurry it up in there, or did you fall down the hole with the rest of the turds?" He stepped out just then, and he was leveling a goddamned Belgian nine-millimeter pinfire revolver at me.

"Wo," I cried, and I throwed myself hard to the right and to the ground, and I hit rolling. I cranked a shell into the chamber of that Winchester, and I spun it around to bear on old Marlin. I heard the hammer on his Belgian six-gun snap just before I fired. His was a misfire. Mine damn near tore off his right arm just below the shoulder.

I had bruised myself up some by that little tactic of mine, but I reckon it was worth it, 'cause I didn't have no bullet in me. Sure, his Belgian thing had missed fire on that one cartridge, but the next one might have tuck. Besides that, I didn't have no way of knowing the damned thing would misfire. I got myself up to my feet and held that Winchester aimed at his gut. "You little bastard," I said, "I ought to go ahead and blow you away."

"Hell, Barjack," he said, "I'm bleeding to death."

I made a gesture with the barrel of my rifle toward the corner of the building.

"Get going," I said. He staggered on around the corner a-clutching at his messed-up shoulder and staggering and whimpering and leaving a trail of blood behind him. I picked up the Belgian pistol and followed him. When he walked through the front door, everyone in there was standing and watching to see what they'd see. The old lady fainted, and the young one gasped. "What in God's name have you done now, Barjack?" Harp demanded, and Ash Face said, "What the hell happened out there?"

I tossed the silly-looking Belgian six-gun over to Ash Face, and he caught it against his belly. "I'd be dead if this damn thing hadn't missed fire on his first shot," I said. "He come out of the outhouse with it."

Ash Face looked over at the station agent. "What do you know about this, Muley?" he said, holding the six-gun out for Muley to look at. Muley walked over closer and leaned over it, squinting his eyes up.

"I never seen it before," he said. "I ain't never even seen one like it." Ash Face looked back at me.

"Any chance he had it hid on him all along?" he asked me.

"Not a chance in hell," I said. "He come right out of my jail cell direct onto the stage. Hell, he never even had any pants on till just before we boarded the stagecoach. That funny-looking son of a bitch was planted out there for him."

"Who could have done it?" Goose Neck asked.

"I'm bleeding to death here," Marlin shouted.

"Shut up," I said. "You brung it all on yourself. You'd be just fine if you hadn't tried to kill me."

"Someone must help him," Harp said, "for Christian charity."

"Well, go on ahead, then," I said. "I don't give a damn. You'll just be saving him for the hangman is all."

66

"Come along, Reverend Harp," said Miss Purdy. "I'll help you."

"What I want to know is who was it what hid that damn Belgian gun out there in the outhouse," I said. And just then I recalled that feller in the crowd back at the county seat giving old Jug a look.

"Four men rode through here this morning," Muley said. "I give them some coffee, and they rode on, but I reckon one of them might have slipped back there with it when I wasn't looking."

"Goddamn it," I said. "Who was they, Marlin?"

But Marlin set up a howl just then. Preacher Harp and Miss Purdy had laid him out on a table and was doing something to him. I seen there wasn't no use trying to talk to him just then. I pulled my flask and tuck a long drink, and then I figured I might just as well get myself something to eat, so I set down and glommed on to a plate. Marlin kept a-howling so that he damned near spoiled my supper, but I et it all, all right, and then I had myself another drink. Ash Face come over and set down beside me.

"Barjack," he said, "you think that someone put that funny-looking six-gun in the outhouse just so old Marlin would find it there?"

"What do you think?" I said. "Does the stage company keep its outhouses outfitted with six-guns?"

"Muley said there was four riders," he said. "If you're right, that means there's four men out there a-looking to get him broke loose from us. That means trouble along the way."

Well, I reckoned that he was sure as hell right about that, and I begun to wonder if getting away from Lil-

lian and the brat was worth all this. I had been lucky
over that misfire, and I had crippled old Marlin good,
but now it looked like there was four more of them
out there, and they was going to be gunning for me
for sure. I tuck another drink. Pretty soon it got quiet.
Old Marlin had quit screaming. "He ain't dead, is he,"
I asked, "or fainted?"

"I hear you, you fat goat," Marlin said, but his
voice wasn't much more than just a whisper.

"Then you tell me," I said, walking over there to
look right down at him in the face. "Who was them
four riders what planted that funny gun out there for
you?"

"Why should I tell you anything, you bastard?" he
sneered at me.

I leaned down real close then and looked him hard
in the eye. " 'Cause if you don't tell me," I said, "I
might just torment that smashed arm of yours somewhat. I might lean on it a little, or I might whop it
with a stick or something."

"You wouldn't do that," he said.

"Barjack," said Harp, "that's inhumane."

"So's getting all our asses killed," I said. There was
a shelf on the wall there beside the table old Jug was
laid out on, and a tin of something or other was setting on it just right up there over his bound-up wound.
I reached over and casual-like tipped that tin off the
shelf, and it fell right on the bloody bandage. God
almighty did he scream and howl, and Harp raved at
me like bloody hell. Miss Purdy put her hands over
her eyes and turned her face away at the same time.

"Pardon me all to hell," I said. "That was damned

clumsy of me. What was I saying? Oh, yeah. Who was them four riders?"

Marlin looked at me like he had never in his whole life wanted to kill anyone so bad as he wanted to kill me right then at that very minute. He snarled and he slavered, and drool run down his chin.

"I'll tell you, then, you son of a bitch," he said. "It was my brother, that's who. My brother and some of his boys. And there's more than just four. There's a bunch of them. That's who it was. It was my brother, and he'll kill all of you. Except you, Miss Purdy. He won't kill you. At least, not right off."

Well, that sure enough sent a chill down my spine, but then I thought that the little bastard might have been lying about the big gang. All we knowed about for sure was just them four. I walked over to Muley and said real low in his ear, "Muley, you got any dynamite around here?"

He said, "No. Ain't got no use for it."

"Hell," I said. "I damn sure do."

"Marlin," said Ash Face. "Marlin. Say, Marlin, what's your brother's name?"

"They call him Snake Eyes," Marlin said, and he grinned through his pain, and then it hit me right smack between the goddamned eyes. Snake Eyes Marlin, better knowed as the Snake Eyes Kid. Why, he was one of the meanest son of a bitches in the whole damned West. A dead shot, they said, and cold-blooded as hell. He was feared and wanted dead or alive just about every damn place on the maps. And here I was dragging his brother all the way across a vast nothing over to Denver to get his ass hanged up to dry, and all the while I'd been pounding on him and starving him and insulting him in ever' way I could think of. Now I'd shot him, too. I knowed they'd want to kill me, and I knowed as well that they'd want to hurt me first. Oh hell, I thought, I'm a dead dog son of a bitch.

Well, then I went and called myself ever' kind of dumb-ass son of a bitch there is. Why in the hell hadn't I thought of it that Jug Marlin would be related to Snake Eyes Marlin? Hell, I had even tuck note of the fact that old Jug had little snake eyes hisself. What a dumb move I had made, and what a deep hole I had dug for myself. Now I couldn't see no way out, and I couldn't see no way of keeping the dirt from being shoveled in on top of me. Maybe, I thought, if I could get the stage turned around and head it back to Asininity fast enough, I could lay in a goddamned good ambush, the way I done for the Bensons that time. Maybe. Dynamite done for them Bensons all right, and it could do as much for the goddamned Marlins. I had me a spark of hope.

"Folks," I said, raising my voice up somewhat, "folks, gather around here and listen up to me a mite. We got ourselves a real problem here. That there prisoner of mine right over there is Jug Marlin, and I just found out just now that his brother is old Snake Eyes Marlin, better known as the Snake Eyes Kid, and in case you ain't heard, he has the worst gang of outlaws this country has ever knowed. There ain't nothing much out there between us and Denver but only a few stage stops here and there and them cold-blooded outlaws a-waiting to pick us off and rescue this worthless bastard. I know they're just after me and him, but the rest of you's going to be in their way when they catch up with us. That is, if we go on."

"Just what do you mean by that, Marshal?" said Preacher Harp.

"I mean that if you was all willing," I said, "we could turn this here stage around and go back where we come from. Then I could put old Marlin there back in my jailhouse in Asininity and wait for his brother and his gang there. The rest of you could catch the next stage out without no Marlin on board and be safe on your trip. Well, what do you say? Believe me, he ain't worth dying for."

"Would we get a refund on our passage money?" old lady Purdy asked.

"I can't say nothing to that," said Goose Neck. "I ain't got the authority to promise that. I ain't even got the authority to turn the stage around."

"But if the rest of us was to insist on it," I said, "I mean all of us, you'll have to, won't you?"

"I don't know," Goose Neck said, scratching his head and wrinkling his old face up. "Maybe."

"Well, we can't afford to take a chance," said the old lady. "We paid our passage, and we mean to be delivered to our destination. Our time of arrival is crucial."

"Now look, lady," I started in to say, but the young one interrupted me.

"She's right, Mr. Barjack," she said. "If we're taking a vote, I vote with my aunt. I vote to go on."

"Well," I said, "I vote we turn back. Pelty, what do you say?"

"I must go on," Van Pelt said. "I have no choice. If I fail in my mission to Denver, I'll lose my job."

"You dumb ass," I said, "if we go on you might lose your silly-ass life, and what good will your job do you then?"

"I vote to go on," he said, clutching his little bag to his chest.

"Preacher?" I said.

"The Lord will protect the righteous," he said.

"You mean the self-righteous, you sanctimonious son of a bitch," I said. "What's your vote?"

"I vote we surge ahead," Harp said. "Onward, always onward. I'd face any number of outlaw armies before I'd again face the Devil's own army in Asininity."

Well hell, I was licked. There wasn't no more I could do. They was all against me. I heard Marlin chuckling over against the wall, and I looked at him and seen his grin. I sudden felt like I was about to piss my pants, and I sure didn't want to be disgraced like that, so I hurried on out back to relieve myself proper. While I set there I wondered about that damned Belgian gun hid in that stinking place. I wondered who done it. Likely, I figured, I'd never know. It was just old Snake Eyes or one of his men. I sure as hell did wish that I had me a few sticks of dynamite, but wishing wasn't doing me no good. I had to think of something else. I had to think of something I could do and not just what I wished I could do. I finished up in there just in time, for the smell was just about to choke me, and I got out and got away from the place before I pulled out my flask. My sup-

ply was getting low already, so I went out to the stage
and opened up the boot and got another bottle out of
my valise and refilled the flask. Then I put the bottle
back, closed up my valise, and retied the boot.

Goose Neck was bringing all the other passengers
out by then, and Preacher Harp was helping old Marlin along. I almost wished that I'd a killed him, but
then we'd a had a stinking corpse on our hands all
the way to Denver. I didn't bother cuffing up old Marlin again. His arm was such a mess, I figured he
wouldn't give me no trouble. It was his brother I was
worried about by then. His brother and all the rest of
them that run with him.

We loaded up and headed out, and I was as nervous
as a field mouse with a red-tailed hawk a-hovering
overhead. Now, I ain't no coward, but I don't believe
in fighting when the odds is all against me, either.
Not if I can figger any other way out of the situation,
and I was figgering as hard as I knowed how. I figgered so hard my head hurt, and then I had me another drink of whiskey to ease it some.

I kept looking out the window to see if I could spot
any riders a-coming, and final I decided that the land
was so damned flat that we wasn't likely to have any
attacks from them for a spell. Likely, I figgered,
they'd wait till there was some cover or someplace to
lay an ambush or something. Out on that flat, if they
was to come at us, why, Ash Face and Goose Neck
would see them coming from a mile away, maybe two
or three. I relaxed a little then, but I knowed that the
trouble was coming sooner or later. I closed my eyes

under my hat brim and tried to get some rest. I knowed I'd need it.

But I didn't get none. My head was swimming with images of about a hundred outlaws riding at us, and me trying to get a bead on just one of them with the stagecoach bouncing around the way it done. And I kept trying to figger a way of evening things up, a way for me to slip up behind them or lay an ambush or something. I couldn't think of nothing. Not a damned thing. I even thought for a minute of asking the preacher to pray for all of us, but then, I knowed that I couldn't bring myself to do that. Maybe I could ask Goose Neck to stop the stage, and then get out and set old Marlin in the road for his brother to pick up, but I rejected that idea 'cause I figgered old Jug would just beg his brother to run me down anyhow so he could get even with me. Well, the short of it is that I never figgered out nothing, and I did eventual drop off to sleep.

When I next woke up, it was dark as hell. It didn't do no good to look out the window. I couldn't have seen no one if he was riding right alongside the coach. I wondered how old Goose Neck could see the road to keep us on it. I couldn't figger out if Snake Eyes and them would attack us in that dark or not, but I sure hoped not. As far as I could tell from the way the stage rolled, we was still on flat land, and I hoped that I was right about them waiting till the landscape changed somewhat.

I could hear snoring all around me. It was like a goddamned symphony. I knowed that I wasn't likely to get no more sleep that night. I felt for my six-guns.

They was right where they was supposed to be, and then I felt for my Winchester and found it still propped there against my left leg. I felt like opening the door and tossing old Marlin out on his ass, but then I knowed that wouldn't do no good neither. Like I said before, they'd just keep after me for what I done to Jug.

Well, I mean to tell you, that was the longest god-damned night I ever spent in my whole entire life. I don't believe I was ever so nervous, neither. And I ain't ashamed to admit that I was real skeered, too. Damn it, there was an army coming after me, and no one but me and two old farts up on the box to fight them off. Hell, I knowed I couldn't count on none of the other passengers. Two women, one wimp, and one preacher what would like nothing better than to send my soul off to hell. Why hell, he'd be more likely to beg God to forgive the son of a bitch what killed me.

So anyhow, it was a hell of a relief when the sun begun to light up the eastern horizon just a little, and then just a little more after that, Goose Neck turned the team off the road. I looked out the window, and I seen that we was headed into another stage stop. I reckoned we'd get ourselfs a breakfast in there, get a little time to stretch our legs, get fresh horses, and then take off again. But then I had me another thought, too. I leaned out the window and yelled up to Goose Neck.

"What you want, Barjack?" he hollered.

"Go in easy," I said. "Remember them four out-laws."

Chapter Six

I heard Ash Face from up on the box say to Goose Neck, "Slow them down, and look careful."

Goose Neck said, "I don't see nobody out." Ash Face said, "Looks like the fresh team's ready."

Goose Neck had slowed the horses almost to a walk and was easing them in to the station. I pushed my door open, tuck up my Winchester, and jumped out. Trotting alongside the stage, I said, "Take her on in, Goose Neck." He did, and I run alongside.

Pretty soon Ash Face yelled out, "There comes old Moon." Then he yelled, "Hey, Moon, everything all right in there?"

Moon called back to him, "Everything's fine and dandy, boys. Roll on in."

I was still suspicious, though, thinking that old Snake Eyes could be right inside with a rifle aimed at old Moon's back or something. I kept myself on the other side of the stage and kept my Winchester ready for action. Goose Neck final stopped the stage, and him and Ash Face clumb down.

"All out, folks," Goose Neck said, opening the door on the side facing the station.

In a low voice I said to Marlin, "You just sit tight, asshole." Ash Face come around to where I was at on the far side, and he was holding his shotgun ready. It was a long double-barreled gun and could do damage at some distance. I was glad for his company.

"I don't see no extra riding horses," he said.

Moon come around to that side about then, and I said, "Moon, is everything for real okay inside?"

"Sure," he said. "What would be wrong? Say. You all looking for some kind of trouble?"

I said, "You see that there ass setting in the coach?" Moon allowed that he did see my prisoner. "That there's Jug Marlin," I said. "His brother is old Snake Eyes. Four of them dropped in to the last station and hid a gun in the outhouse. As you can see, that scheme didn't work too good, but them four is out there somewheres. Maybe more of them."

"I'll be damned," Moon said. "I bet it was them four that rode through here last night."

"Last night?" I said, like a dumb ass. "Tell us about them."

"Ain't much to tell," Moon said. "They was four of them, like you said. Looked like drifters to me. They et a meal and paid me for it. Asked what time the stage was due through here, and then they rode on."

77

"Which way?" I asked.

Moon pointed toward Denver. "West," he said.

I relaxed a little and lowered my Winchester, and I noticed that Ash Face done the same way with his gun. "Well," I said, "I reckon we can get on with business. Get your ass out of there, Marlin." Marlin went and crawled out the other side.

"Breakfast's ready inside," Moon said.

"Thanks," said Ash Face. I headed for the house, but I seen Marlin going around back.

"Hey, Marlin," I hollered. He stopped and looked over his shoulder.

"I need to go out back," he said.

"Wait for me," I said. I caught up with him and passed him by on my way to the outhouse. When I jerked open the door, Preacher Harp was setting there.

His eyes popped wide, and he said, "Barjack! This is an outrage."

I said, "It sure smells like one. Hell, I didn't know preachers had to do that too."

I shut the door and stood back, waiting for the preacher to get his business done.

When he final come out, he just stalked by me like he was mad as several badgers. I tuck me a deep breath and held it, then looked inside. I didn't see nothing out of the ordinary, but I went on and stepped inside. I still didn't see nothing, and my wind was about to give out on me, so I turned around to leave, and then I seen it. It was a Smith & Wesson this time, one of them kind that breaks in half, and it was stuck up over the door. I had to stretch myself to reach it, but I tuck it down. Then I stepped outside and sucked in a big breath of fresh air. I held the six-gun out for Marlin to see.

"This here what you was looking for?" I asked him.

"Why, no, hell," he said. "I just needed to . . . you know."

"Well, go on, then," I said.

"I—I don't need—"

"You said you needed to go in there," I told him. "Go on in."

"It can wait," he said.

I cocked that Smith & Wesson and aimed it right at his crotch, and I kind of enjoyed the horrified look that come on his face. "Go on in there," I said, and he did. "Shut the door," I said. He did, but he looked awful reluctant. I tuck out a cigar and fired it up. There was a tree stump a couple of feet away from me, so I went over and set myself down on it to enjoy a good smoke. I leaned my Winchester across my left leg and pulled out my flask and had me a drink. Then I put the flask away again and set there enjoying my smoke. By and by I heard Marlin's voice real whiny-like.

"Barjack?" he said. "Barjack, can I come out of here?" I never answered him, so he whined out again, "Barjack, I'm gagging to death. Can I come out?"

"You needed to go," I said. "Stay there and get your business done."

"I'm all done, Barjack," he whimpered. "Please let me come out."

Well, I thought about that breakfast inside and how if the others didn't eat it all up from me, what was left would get cold if I didn't get my ass in there, so

I give in. "Come on, Marlin," I said, and I never seen anyone respond to anything so damn quick. He come out of that little house like he'd been blowed out by dynamite. He like to fell on his face, but he managed to catch hisself and stay on his feet. He was sure gasping for air. Final he said, "Man, that preacher sure left a powerful stink in there."

"That's the way with preachers," I said. "Come on."

We went inside and had ourselves a pretty good meal. I showed the Smith & Wesson to Ash Face and Goose Neck. We knowed that them four was still out there somewheres ahead of us just a-waiting for the right chance. I made another speech begging ever'one to turn around and go back, but it was a waste of time, so I told myself that was it. That was my last chance. The farther along the way we got, the more sure it was that we was going to go all the way—at least until old Snake Eyes stopped us.

We wound up hanging around old Moon's station for quite a spell. Ever'one needed to make use of the outhouse, and it tuck a while for it to kind of clear out old Harp's stench. We let the ladies use it first then, in case any of us was to leave as foul an odor as had the preacher. We all used it, though, 'cause we knowed that it was twelve miles on down the road to the next station. I made old Marlin wait to the very last, though, before I'd let him go in there again.

Pretty soon we was rumbling along the damn rough road again. I swear that was the worst traveling I ever done. On a stagecoach you're bouncing up and down and being jounced from side to side all the damn time.

There ain't no relief. If there's other passengers, as there almost always is, you're knocking into one another constant. It was a good thing for us that old Pelty was clutching his little bag so close, 'cause if there's any loose baggage on the inside, it can get slung around something fierce.

My ass was dead and sore from all the bouncing, and from just setting on that bench all that long. My legs was stiff, and so was my back. I was damn drowsy, too, 'cause you for sure can't hardly sleep under the kind of circumstances what I've been describing to you. And then there's the dust what you're constantly breathing up your nostrils and into your mouth. Old Pelty got to coughing a bit from that, and both ladies was holding hankies to their faces. What I'm telling you is that, if I had to have got out of that goddamned stagecoach and try to take on a bunch of owlhoots, well, hell, I might not even have been able to stand up on my own feet. I was miserable, and I was damn nervous about the future.

But even bouncing around like we was, a body can still think. And I got started thinking about the other passengers, 'cause I was mad at them all for voting against me on the matter of turning the stagecoach around. I was just thinking how mad I was at them when the question come to my mind of how come they all voted against me. It seemed to me that my position was a damned intelligent one. Turn around and go back to safety before Marlin's gang could catch up with us. Then take the next stage west. Jug Marlin would be back in my jail, and the next stage wouldn't be in no danger 'cause of his presence. I couldn't figure why they wouldn't go along with that.

Goose Neck and Ash Face hadn't actually voted. 'Course, Goose Neck had said that he didn't have no authority to turn a stagecoach around, and he had his schedule to keep. But that wasn't really a vote. I reckoned that if ever' single passenger had voted to go on back, why, he'd a done it. So I didn't really consider that them two stage company employees had voted, and so I wasn't really mad at them. And old Jug, he didn't count for nothing neither. 'Course, if I'd a let him vote, he'd a voted with the others against me, 'cause he for sure wanted us to ride smack into his brother's gang of badasses.

It was the other ones I was mad at and couldn't figger out. The preacher hadn't said nothing but that he didn't want to go back to the sinful town of Asininity. I could have accepted that all right under any other circumstances, but with death ahead and Asininity behind, I couldn't figger the preacher. Why, hell, he wouldn't even have had to go all the way back to Asininity. He could get off there at the county seat. I figgered that maybe he had some other reason for wanting to keep on.

And the women. I'd a figgered them to be scared into turning around, but they voted to go on. They said they was afraid of losing their tickets. I couldn't quite buy that neither. And then there was old Pelty. He had said that he was skeered of losing his job. I couldn't hardly believe that wimpy little runt was brave enough to face the trouble what almost sure for certain lay ahead of us. So anyhow, I got to wondering what their secret real reasons was. I figgered that each one of them must have such a secret real reason. Once curiosity gets ahold of you like that, it's hard to shrug it off. Right then my brain commenced to being occupied with that question almost as much as with the problem of how I was going to keep myself alive whenever old Snake Eyes at last come to make his move.

At the next stop I was the first one into the outhouse, and by God if I didn't find a sawed-off shotgun behind the door. They was still ahead of us all right, and still trying to fix things so that old Jug might be able to make his own break. I tuck the gun out and showed it to him. He said, "So you got that move figured out. It don't matter, Barjack. My brother's going to get you sooner or later. And if you're still alive after the fight, he'll let me kill you personal, and I'm going to take my time and really enjoy it, too." No one was looking, so I just kind of slapped him on the hurt shoulder with the barrel of that little shotgun. He yowled out something fierce, and I reckon it must have hurt like hell. I think if a real doctor had got a look at him, that arm would a come off.

"I've made up my mind about something, Marlin," I said. He was still whimpering, but he managed to ask me, "Whut?"

"Out there in Denver," I said, "whenever they put that noose around your neck to test out how heavy your ass is, I am going to be there watching."

We went on inside for cups of hot coffee while the horses was getting changed outside. It wasn't noon yet, so they wasn't no meal. It would be a fairly short stop. Anyhow, the fellow inside asked old Goose

Neck, "Has you got a Marlin amongst your passengers?" I shot a hard glance at Marlin, and he kept his yap shut.

"Well, yeah," said Goose Neck. I stepped up right quick.

"I'm Marshal Barjack," I said. "What's your interest in this Marlin?"

The old boy said to me then, "I ain't got no interest, Marshal, but a little while ago four riders come in here. They give me this here note and asked me to hand it over to a Marlin what would be on the coach coming through."

I said, "I'll take it." He handed me the note, and I read through it real quick. Then I give it to old Goose Neck, and Ash Face crowded up next to him to read over his shoulder.

It said: "Jug, we tried to help you out along the way but it looks like it ain't worked so far. In case this one don't work, we'll be waiting for you in the hills. There's me and Justin and Dewey and the Swede. Your brother's waiting for us at No Name." And it was signed, "Orvel."

I looked over at Marlin, and I said, "Who's Orvel?"

"Orvel Hooper," he said. "He's one of my brother's boys. He's just about the fastest man alive with a six-gun, I reckon. If Orvel's out there, you're a dead man, Barjack."

"Justin?" I said.

Marlin grinned real wide. "Justin Long. He's pretty good with his guns too," he said, "but he really likes to cut people. Likely he'll ask Orvel not to kill ever'one so he'll be able to do some cutting."

"Dewey?" I said.

"Reckon that'd be old Dewey Decker," he said. "Last count I knew, Dewey was wanted for twelve killings."

"And Swede?" I said.

"Swede's good with his guns," Marlin said. "He don't like six-guns so much. He'd rather shoot a rifle. Prefers a Henry. But Swede's a brawler. He likes to fight with his fists. I believe he could wrassle a grizzly bear down. He's a tough son of a bitch. Uh, pardon me, Reverend, ladies. His name is Ole something or other. I can't recall. We just always call him Swede. Hell, Barjack, them's my brother's best men. I'd sure hate to be in your boots just now."

I sidled over to Goose Neck then, and I asked him, "What's this place called No Name where old Snake Eyes is waiting for us?"

"It's a little place about forty miles this side of Denver," Goose Neck said. "It's our last home station before we go on into Denver. They's three more swing stations, like this one, between No Name and Denver, but No Name's the last home station. It's got a little settlement growed up around it, but it ain't a real town. Got a saloon and some . . . you know, some ladies. Couple of stores, a stable. Just the basics, you know."

I carried the note over to Marlin and handed it to him. "Your pal Orvel has done us a favor," I said. "Now we know pretty well what to expect and where to expect it. Hell, your brother ain't even out here. He just sent some of his underlings is all."

"Them 'underlings,' as you call them, is enough to

take care of the likes of you," Marlin said. "Hell, you won't even get a chance to meet Snake Eyes."

"I'll meet him," I said. "I'll be the last thing he sees in this life." But to tell you the truth, I wasn't really near so confident as I was making out, and even if I was to figger a way to get old Snake Eyes, I didn't intend that he would ever see me, for I ain't no fool. Going face-to-face against a gunfighter is just about the stupidest thing a man can do. My intention was to find my way around behind him and see how good a target his back would be. A man with good sense can take out the best gunfighter in the world that way. Hell, look what that little dip Jack McCall done to Wild Bill Hickok.

Goose Neck said, "We're ready to roll, Barjack. Can we load them up?"

"Yeah," I said. "I'm ready."

In just a little bit, we was out on the road again. I noticed that the preacher wasn't hounding me no more, and I got to thinking that I hadn't heard him say nary a word since he had left such a big stink back at that one station. I reckon he had embarrassed himself. I thought about trying to comfort him some by telling him that if God made us all, he made us with the stink a part of us, and so it wasn't nothing to be ashamed of, but I decided that he likely wouldn't appreciate that kind of remark none, so I kept quiet. I was just glad that he was keeping his big mouth shut for a change.

Actual, all of us had got pretty quiet since we had learned that there was for real four outlaws out there somewhere ahead of us just a-waiting to catch us off guard. I leaned my head out the window to look ahead and see what kind of terrain was up there. Things still looked to be wide and flat and bare. I settled back down. It would be just about twelve miles to the next swing station. I figgered we'd be all right till then. I pulled out my flask and tuck a slug, and by God, I went to sleep.

I woke up when Goose Neck was turning into the next station, and I got myself alert again real quick. I stuck my neck out again and hollered up to him, "What's it look like?"

He told me, "I don't see no riding horses. Bemis is out with the fresh team. Looks okay to me."

I settled back down, but I kept my hands on my gun handles. In another minute we was all unloaded again, and once again I went to check the outhouse. This time there wasn't no gun in there. I guess they had final got the notion that I wasn't going to fall for that trick.

Bemis and Goose Neck was changing the horses, and the passengers was all taking their turns at the outhouse, and then getting hot coffee on the inside of the station. I searched out Ash Face.

"What's it like ahead of here?" I asked him.

"It starts to get a little hilly a few miles ahead," he said. "Kind of rolling hills, you know, and clumps of trees here and there."

I said, "Good places to set up an ambush, huh?"

He said, "Could be."

"Ash Face," I said, "if them four hits us, it's only going to be just you and me. You know that, don't you? The preacher and the banker and them two ladies ain't going to be worth a damn, and Goose Neck's going to be busy driving."

"I been thinking on that," he said.

"And if we're running," I said, "I ain't going to be much good inside the coach. I'm thinking maybe I ought to climb up on top with you."

"Sounds like a good idea to me, Barjack," he said. "I'll tell Goose Neck."

Then I walked over to where old Harp was sipping on a cup of coffee. "Preacher," I said, "I know you'd just as soon not talk to me ever again, but I got to ask you a question, even though I think I know the answer already."

He stiffened up and said, "Ask it, then."

"Are you carrying about your person any kind of concealed weapon?" I said.

"Of course not," he said. "I'm a man of God."

"Well," I said, "so was Gideon, I reckon, and little David, but that's all right."

I made my way over to the ladies and asked them the same question, and they said that no they wasn't, and then I asked wimpy little Van Pelt, and he also said no. I didn't think that none of them would be, but, you see, I was thinking that I was going to leave my prisoner alone in the coach with them, and so I had to be sure. He wouldn't be worth much if he tried to start anything, not with his one arm damn near shot off, and that his right arm too, but I didn't want to take no chances. Well, right after that old Goose Neck called us all aboard.

We was loading up when Ash Face come over to me.

"I had me a thought, Barjack," he said.

"Tell me," I said. "I sure ain't had a good one in a while."

He leaned in kind of close, and he said, "What if we was to put old Marlin there up on top too? You reckon that might slow his pals down somewhat for fear they might hit him by mistake?"

"By God," I said, "Ash Face, that's a hell of a good idea. Let's do it."

Chapter Seven

Well, we was bouncing along on that goddamned rough old road and rolling down into a kind of valley with clumps of trees here and there along the sides and some piles of boulders and such, and I had old Marlin handcuffed by his left wrist to the rails what run around the top to keep the baggage in place, and I was setting there right behind him with my Winchester in my hand. I was trying to watch all around, up ahead, on both sides and behind us, but I wasn't keeping up with all that too good. I noticed that old Ash Face, he didn't move his head at all. He was just watching right up in front of us. Of a sudden, I heard him yell.

"Barjack," he said. "Straight ahead."

Well, I swung around to look, and sure enough, there they was all strung out across the road. They

was four of them, all right, and right away I figgered
it had to be them four members of old Snake Eyes's
gang. Two of them was holding six-guns ready, and
two was holding rifles.

"Keep them rolling," I yelled. I knowed that Ash
Face and Goose Neck made pretty good targets up
there on the box, but that's how come we was counting on old Jug Marlin being a kind of deterrent up on
top. I grabbed Jug by the hair of his head and pulled
him up tall and shoved him kind of between Ash Face
and Goose Neck.

"Show yourself, goddamn you," I yelled into the
side of his head.

I leveled my Winchester by laying it over his
shoulder. I was kind of using him for a shield, you
see. And I popped off a shot. I think I might have
tore off an ear with that shot, 'cause I seen one of the
bastards drop his six-gun and grab the side of his
head, and I heard him yelp. The other three looked
like they was thinking about shooting back, but then
they hesitated, and then they run to the side of the
road. I figure that they must have recognized old Jug
up there on top. A stray shot could have got Jug, you
see, and they sure didn't want that to happen. Well,
the guy who was holding his head was the last one
standing in the road, and he looked right at us a-
coming right at him, and he made like he was going
to pick his shooter up from the ground, and then he
looked up again and seen how fast we was coming,
and then he run—without the shooter.

We raced right on past there and just kept a-going,
and I thought that I was going to get bounced right

off the top of that goddamned stagecoach. I hung on tight to old Jug, figuring that if I was to get flung off, I could use him to climb back up over, 'cause at least he'd be dangling by one wrist. I did manage to look back, though, and I seen them four come back out into the road and look after us. A couple of them fired shots, but I think they fired high on purpose. Like I said, they didn't want to take no chances on hitting old Jug by mistake. Well, I begun to think that was a pretty damn good idea old Ash Face had got about putting Jug up there. The only problem was that it was awful discomforting setting up there on top like that. Not for Jug. I didn't give a damn about his discomfort. It's my own beat-up ass that was worrying me. Still, it was better than getting killed.

"They ain't done," Jug said. "They ain't give up yet."

"Shut up, asshole," I said.

I knowed he was right, though. I knowed they'd try again. Now that they knowed how old Jug was stuck up there on top to give them the worries, they'd be prepared for it on their next try. They knowed now that they would have to pick their shots real careful-like. It was certain possible, and I knowed that too, to lay down somewheres and just wait and take a real careful aim and then pick off the driver or the shotgun and not hit someone else by mistake. What we had done back there was that we had surprised them by showing Jug up on top, and they hadn't had no time to think on it. Likely they had figgered that when we seen them across the road like that, we'd just stop, and even if we didn't, they figured they'd just blast away real crazy-like at anyone and everyone up there on the box. Then they seen Jug, and that fuddled their brains just momentary-like. Well, I knowed it wouldn't happen like that again.

I figgered they had two choices, maybe three. They could get on their horses and chase us. They could catch up pretty easy, and then they could try to pick us off at a run or ride right up alongside us to get some close shots or even try to board us. 'Course, if they tried it like that, they would for sure be in danger of hitting old Jug by accident, 'cause getting in a careful shot from the back of a running horse ain't the easiest thing in the world to do. Still, they might try it.

Or they could mount up and ride lickety-split till they was to get well ahead of us and then find them a good spot and lay in an ambush. Like I done said, a good man with a rifle hid snug up behind a boulder could pretty easy knock off at least one of the two men on the box, maybe both. If that was to happen, why, I'd have to try to get hold of the reins and manage the team, and if I was to do that, then I'd be an easy target up there. That seemed to me like a probable next move on their part.

The last possibility that come into my mind was that they might just ride on ahead to that there place called No Name and report to old Snake Eyes just what the situation was, and then they'd all be just a-waiting for us to roll in there. Well, there wasn't nothing for it but for us to keep our eyes open and watch all around the way we had been doing. The only thing we knowed for sure that we hadn't knowed before was that the four bastards was behind us now.

'Course, we didn't know how long they'd stay back there. They could maybe get around us somewhere off the road, and we wouldn't know it till they started blasting.

About that time I was thinking about how comfy everything was back home in Asininity, and I don't think it even come in my head just then how bitchy old Lillian had become nor even what a little snot-nosed brat my kid was. Mostly I was asking myself why in hell old Happy had chose of all the towns in the whole wide West to bring Jug Marlin into my town and thereby bring all this uncalled-for misery down on my undeserving head and shoulders. I told myself that the next time I ever seen Happy, if I was still alive, I ought to punch him a good one up to the side of his jaw for this. I was calling him all kinds of stupid for not knowing or figgering out that Jug Marlin was the brother of Snake Eyes Marlin. And it was just about then that I seen them coming up behind us, riding like hell, all four of them. I gouged Ash Face in the back, and he turned and looked, and then he elbowed Goose Neck. Goose Neck tuck a quick look, and then he really whipped up them horses. Jug like to have fell off the stage, but he never, and I laid myself down flat with my Winchester aimed back at those sons of bitches. They was a little far back for a shot yet, what with all the bouncing and jouncing and the road being curvy and rolling the way it was.

Old Jug must have got nervous thinking about all the shooting that was fixing to commence, so he went and laid down too. I seen him, and I yelled up to Ash Face. "Stick that shotgun up Jug's ass and blow his pants off if he don't set up tall." That shotgun wasn't no good at that range nohow, and I couldn't see a better use for it. So Ash Face done what I said, and Jug for sure set up right tall. I turned all my attention back to our four pursuers. One was getting about in range of my Winchester.

Now, I ain't never been one to be cruel to dumb animals on purpose, but on the other hand, I ain't never seen no profit in being overly sentimental when my own survival is at stake. A moving target is a tough one to hit under any circumstances, and when the shooter is bouncing up and down and swinging from side to side, it's even worse. And a man is a much smaller target than a horse. If you'll put all that information together, you'll understand why I done what I done. I tuck a real careful aim, and as soon as I thought I could make my shot, I fired, and I dropped that lead horse.

Well, it screamed real loud and sounded almost human, and its front legs buckled, and its head come down and hit the dirt, and its ass end come flying up over its head. If my shot didn't kill it, then it had to have broke its neck falling the way it done, and when it fell, it tossed the rider way out ahead of its own self, and he hit hard and never moved again that I could see. Hell, I figured that one shot had likely caused two broke necks. I think he was the same one whose ear I think I had shot off.

"Good shot, Barjack," Ash Face yelled.

The other three slowed down a mite, as if they was thinking whether or not they should ought to stop and see about the one that was shot down, but one of them hollered something and waved his arm, and they just kept on a-riding after us just leaving him lay there for the buzzards. They either figured he was done dead, or else they just didn't give a damn one way or the other. I made myself ready for another shot. I was hoping they would just keep on like that after I seen what I could do. Just about then the stagecoach swerved sharp to the right, and old Jug fell over and landed across my legs. He also landed on his bad shoulder, and that must of hurt like billy hell, 'cause he sure did scream out. Ash Face shoved his shotgun right up Jug's ass, and Jug set back up real quick-like.

I lost sight of the three riders then till the road straightened up a mite, and then I seen them come on around the bend. One of them had his rifle up at his shoulder, and he was riding without holding the reins. I couldn't recollect which one of the four Jug had said was a dead shot with the rifle, but it must have been him, and I don't know if he was an old buffalo runner or what. Maybe it was just a lucky shot, but he squeezed one off riding along like that, and by God, it tore into old Goose Neck's shoulder. Goose Neck howled out and grabbed for his shoulder and dropped the lines.

I pulled my trigger, and killed myself another horse, and the son of a bitch what had shot Goose Neck went flying through the air. I seen him hit hard and bounce, and I seen the other two pull up beside him. I didn't know if that meant that he was still alive, or that they cared more about him than the last one, or they thought that the odds had been trimmed down too much for them. But they had stopped, and we was running wild. I turned around and crawled up close to the box.

"I lost the lines," Goose Neck said.

"Hell," I said, "I can see that. What the hell are we going to do?"

"We're going to wreck," he said.

Ash Face said, "We got to get the lines."

"How the hell're we going to do that?" I said.

"One of us has got to climb down there after them," he said.

"Well," I said, "go on, then."

Ash Face looked at me like he thought that I was crazy or something. "Look down there, Barjack," he said. "I'd as soon take my chances on getting flung off when this thing turns over."

I crawled on forward a little and looked down. The lines was dragging along between the horses, and the stage was bouncing along fast and out of control. It was hitting rocks and ruts and being throwed up high, and it was swinging wildly from side to side. It looked like that ground beneath us was just a-flying backwards down there, and if a man was to fall down there, why, he'd get chewed up and spit out behind, and what was left of him would look like something you might see hanging on a hook in the butcher's shop. I seen what Ash Face was talking about.

Then I looked ahead a little. If I couldn't get to the lines, the next thing would be to get to the horses. But I never before realized just how far it is from the coach to the rearmost horse's ass. Goddamn, it looked a far piece of space with nothing in it but a bouncing,

swinging wooden tongue and the fast-moving hard
and rocky ground. I considered old Ash Face's alter-
native of getting flung off the top when the goddamned stagecoach was to turn over, which it was most
bound to do if this kept up much longer, and I looked
off to the side. That didn't seem like too good a prospect to me neither. Either way, I figured, I'd be dead,
and I ain't afraid to die, I just ain't never wanted to
rush it along none.

Well, I called myself seven kinds of a damn fool,
and I handed my Winchester to old Ash Face, and I
went and clumb off the top over onto the box. I set
there a minute a-looking at the place where I was
foolish enough to think that I was a-going. I thought
about sidling down the front of the box till I could
get my feet on that bouncing tongue, but it come to
me that I might could slip and land astraddle of that
damn thing and mash my privates. I tuck a good aim
at the ass end of the rearmost left-hand horse, and
then I closed my eyes and flung my own ass out into
the air.

Well, by God, if I didn't land on it. It plumb near
knocked all the wind out of me, for I was laying out
on it on my belly with my arms and legs both splayed
out onto both its sides. My fingers went to groping
right away till I had caught hold of the harness straps,
and I'm here to tell you that I gripped them hard. It
wasn't near like setting a saddle, but it was a more
secure feeling than being on top of that wild running
stagecoach.

I caught my breath a little, and then I pulled myself
up into a setting position, and I just rode that horse

for a spell, and I tried to slow him down, but I seen real soon that it wasn't no use. I knowed that I'd have to make my way somehow up to one of them lead animals.

Well, I started looking to see some way I could move, and I figgered that I could likely brave myself up some and get over to the back of the horse to my right, but then I couldn't really see no advantage in that. I'd still just be riding along on the back of one of the rear horses. The problem was how to move ahead. I couldn't hardly crawl over the horse's neck and head to get to the next one's ass. The only way was to move along between the horses. I looked down at that tree running right down the middle, and it sure didn't look none too substantial to me, and I don't believe that I have ever in my whole life felt myself moving along so fast as what I was then. I can tell you that I was in a hell of a spot.

Just then I seen a rider moving hard and fast alongside of us. He was whipping at his horse like he was some desperate to get somewhere. At first I thought that he must be one of old Snake Eyes's gang, and I sure wasn't in no position to defend myself, but then I noticed that he wasn't toting no firearms. He kept right beside us and kept riding hard till he come up just even with the right-hand lead horse, and then, by God, he reached over and tuck ahold of that lead horse's flying mane, and he just drug hisself out of his saddle and on over onto the back of that other horse. I swear to God I ain't never seen nothing like it before or since, and then pretty soon, why, he had managed to get that wild-ass team of six horses stopped.

Well, he got down, and he calmed them horses down some. Then he gathered up the lines and handed them up to Goose Neck. He seen, just then, I guess, that Goose Neck was bleeding, and he asked him, "Can you drive this thing?"

Goose Neck said, "I ain't sure."

The stranger clumb up beside him then. I slid myself down off the wild back I had been a-riding, and my legs like to buckled under me, but I managed to stay up.

That feller looked down at me, and he said, "Will you bring my saddle horse?" I was glad to oblige.

Well, he drove that stage a little on down the road till he come to a spot wide enough to turn her around, and then he started back the other way. I rode easy alongside. In a little ways, I seen a station, and I realized then that we had rode hard right by our next swing stop and never knowed the difference. Leastways I sure hadn't noticed. That feller pulled the stage to a stop, and I stopped his horse and dropped myself down to the ground. I made my way right quick for the outhouse, but this time I wasn't looking for no gun.

When I had done my chore, I stood out back of the station for just a bit till I had damn near emptied my flask. Then I walked back around the building. I seen the stranger changing the horses, and from up on top of the stage, old Jug yelled at me.

"Barjack," he said, "let me down from here. I'm about to mess my pants." Well, I knowed he wasn't lying, so I went and let him loose. He hurried for the back side of the building, looking some desperate. I figgered there wasn't no harm in him with that messed-up shoulder and no weapon, so I just went on over to the stage boot and refilled my flask. Then I went inside.

I found Ash Face tending to Goose Neck's arm. I walked over to them, and I asked, "How is it?"

Ash Face said, "It ain't too bad." And Goose Neck said, "I'll be all right. Hell, I shouldn't never have dropped them lines, but it tuck me so by surprise."

I asked him, "Are you going to be able to drive with that?"

He said, "Yeah. Sure. I'm all right."

I went on over to the table and poured myself a cup of coffee and set down. The preacher was setting at the table looking white as a cloth on the table at the White Owl Supper Club in Asininity. Van Pelt was clutching his bag up close to his chest and just staring straight ahead. The Purdy ladies was comforting each other.

Marlin come in then, looking somewhat relieved. He looked at me some sheepish, and he said, "Can I get myself some of that coffee?" I told him to go on ahead, and then the stranger come in. I met him face-to-face and stuck out my right hand, and he shuck it all right. He had a right firm grip, too.

"I'm Marshal Barjack," I said. "You sure come along at just the right time to save our ass. Just how come you to be so handy like that?"

"Sam Longstreet," he said. "I run the station here. I was waiting for you with a fresh team, and I seen you run past. I'd a been along sooner, but I had to saddle up a horse. What happened out there, anyhow?"

I told Longstreet all about my prisoner and the four outlaws out there, and how now there was only two of them. At least there was only two horses. I didn't really know what shape the second horseless man was in. I only knowed that I'd unhorsed him. I also knowed that they was still back there behind us. That made me think that maybe Longstreet was in some danger. If there was still three live outlaws with only two horses, they might figger old Longstreet's stop would be a good place to get theirselves another horse. I told him that, and he said, "I'll be watching for them." I figured he was a man what could handle hisself all right, special if he knowed ahead of time that there was likely to be trouble a-coming.

I reckon that I had still not really got over our experience out there on the road, for all of a sudden I had a powerful impulse to have myself another drink. I pulled out my flask and tuck a long suck on it. Then, recalling my manners and the way in which old Longstreet had saved my ass and everyone else's, I offered it to him, and he accepted and had hisself a snort. I was glad of that, for I had tuck a liking to the man. It's hard not to do that when a man has saved your ass for you.

I was feeling somewhat better, and just then old Harp got his voice back, I guess, for he piped up and said, "Marshal Barjack, I must register a strong protest. You have endangered all of our lives needlessly and shamefully. It's bad enough that you endangered my life and that of Mr. Van Pelt, but there were two helpless ladies with us in that coach. Only the grace of God saved us all from being killed, either by bullets or by being broken to bits in a terrible crash. I—"

I interrupted the son of bitch then by breaking in on his harangue. "I warned all of you of the danger," I said, "and I tried to get you to turn back. It's too late now. We're too far along, but you all wanted to continue this trip even after I told you about the Snake Eyes gang. Now that what I warned you about has done actual happened, you start in to bellyaching. And by the way, Preacher, it wasn't God saved our ass, it was Mr. Longstreet here. You had really ought to thank him for that."

"Be that as it may, Marshal," Harp said, "you have no right to put us in further danger."

"I done told you," I said, "we're too far along to turn back now. Just what the hell do you expect me to do?"

"When the stagecoach pulls out of here," he said, "I expect you and your prisoner to remain behind."

Chapter Eight

"You brimstone-slinging son of a bitch," I said, "I got me a prisoner to deliver to a United States marshal, a murdering bastard son of a yellow dog, and he's got a brother out there with a whole gang of the meanest hoot owls in the whole entire West, just a-waiting to turn him loose on the innocent population of those decent folks you like to harp on so much. Harp, you can talk all you want about decent men, but any real man would get a gun and do his damndest to see that I get this bastard delivered up safe to the hangman."

"I protest this language," said the preacher, and I guess he should've, 'cause I turned on my goddamndest cussing powers against that phony. I can't hardly stomach a phony bastard and a hypocrite. Now, someone like old Jug Marlin, you can shoot him in the back of the head and forget about it, but them damn phonies, you can't kill them and get away with it, and you can't beat any sense of honesty into their heads neither. All you can do is just put up with them or · cuss them. That's all. I had done reminded them of their vote to go on in spite of my talking sense to them about the danger that was a-waiting for us along the way. There wasn't no sense I could see in bringing that up again. But I did have another thought.

"What I'd like to know," I said, "is what makes each one of you folks so all-fired anxious to get away from where you was getting away from to wherever it is you plan to get yourself to. And Preacher, since you was the one what started all this jawing, suppose you start off."

"What do you mean?" Harp said.

"Tell me again," I said, "and tell all these folks here how come you was so anxious to keep this coach rolling west even when you knowed there was a chance we'd all get ourselves killed. Come on. Tell us."

"I don't have to tell you anything," Harp said. "I answer only to God."

"Then I'll tell the rest of them just what it was you told me before," I said. "What he said was that he was a-leaving Asininity 'cause no one would go to church. He said that he didn't have no flock to tend back there. Well, all right. I can accept that. But then we rode on over to the county seat. He could've stayed there, couldn't he? And whenever we seen that them outlaws was out here laying for us, and I suggested we turn around and go back, he was against it. How come does he think it's better to maybe get hisself killed than to wait back at the county seat for another coach?"

Harp folded his arms across his chest and rared back. "I answer only to my God," he said.

"Yeah?" I said, and then I turned on the others. "And what about the rest of you? Is your lousy bank job more important than your life, Pelty? Your job and those damn papers you keep hugging?" Van Pelt just hugged the bag tighter and looked at the ground. "And you ladies?" I said. I reached out sudden on an impulse and jerked away old lady Purdy's handbag from her. She shrieked at me and reached for it, but I turned my back on her real quick and opened that purse. I rummaged a little, and then I come up with a handful of bills, and they wasn't all small ones, neither. I pulled them out and held them up for everyone to see. "Looky here," I said. "The ladies said they wanted to keep going 'cause they couldn't afford another passage, and they didn't know if the stage line would give them a refund. Look at this. Hell, they could afford to pay all our passage."

I stuffed the money back into the bag and give it back to the old lady, who snatched it out of my hand and give me a real walrus-faced look. "You're despicable," she said.

"I don't rightly know what that means," I said, "but I reckon I probably am." I looked over at Miss Purdy, but she only just blushed and ducked her head. "Well," I said, "since no one wants to talk, I'll say something. I mean to deliver my goddamned prisoner. I ain't staying here neither to wait for no other stage or to get killed here by them outlaws. You all voted to go on ahead, and we're going on ahead. All of us. And that's the end of that."

"Marshal Barjack," said Harp, and he had a hell of a smug look on his face, "must I remind you that you are only a town marshal? And we're far from your town? You're well out of your jurisdiction, Marshal. You have no authority whatever over any of us."

"Well, now, Preacher," I said, "under ordinary everyday circumstances, you might be right about that, but I just happen to be transporting Marlin under direct orders from a United States marshal. And that makes all the diddly damn difference."

Ash Face said, "There's meal on the table, and if we don't get at it right now, it ain't going to be fit to eat." Well, that shut us all up for a while. We set down to stuff our faces, and I realized that I was for sure damned hungry too. I et till there was nothing left on the platters to eat. The others all done theirselves pretty proud too, even the ladies. I had myself another cup of coffee, and then I tuck another swig from my flask for good measure.

Harp then said, "Am I to take it, Marshal, that you still insist on riding along with us?"

"I done said all I mean to say about it, Preacher," I said.

"I don't know about all this argufying," Goose Neck said of a sudden, "but I got to get rolling. I got a schedule to keep. If you're going with me, get aboard."

We all went outside headed for the coach, and then damned if I didn't see old Longstreet come a-riding in toward us and leading another horse. It come to me then than I hadn't noticed him around for a spell. We all stood there a-waiting for him to ride on in and see what the hell he'd been up to. He come in closer, and I seen that there was two bodies slung across that extra horse. Right close to me, he stopped.

"I got two of them for you, Barjack," he said.

"Hey, Preacher," I called out. "That calm you down some?" I turned back to Longstreet. "Hell," I said, "I didn't even know you was gone till I saw you riding back. That's damn good work, partner. Fast, too."

Old Longstreet swung hisself down out of the saddle. "It wasn't too much trouble," he said. "You had them figured right. They were headed right here, almost for sure looking for another horse. When they saw me coming, one of them took a shot. There were two of them riding one horse, and I took a rifle shot and got them both with one bullet. That's these here. The other one took off fast. I trailed him a little ways. Last I saw of him, he was riding straight west as hard as he could go."

"Well," I said, "he could be riding up ahead to try to ambush us again, but I doubt it. Not all by his lonesome. And that after three of his buddies has been killed. Most likely he's headed for No Name to tell old Snake Eyes what's happened. I'm obliged to you, Longstreet. When I come back through here, we'll have us another drink together."

"I'll be looking forward to it, Barjack," he said. He was a man's man and a real gentleman, that Longstreet, and what he had done for us relaxed me more than I got words to say, for even if that last outlaw was to choose to lay in another ambush for us, why, he was only one where they had been four.

I tied the outlaw's horse onto the back end of the stage, and we loaded on up and headed on out, and ever'one was quiet for a ways down the road. Once again, me and Marlin was riding inside with the rest of the passengers. And Marlin was not only quiet, he was sort of stunned. He just stared ahead at nothing, and it come to me that he was a man for the first time since he had slipped in that dog puke what realized actual and for real that he was getting closer and closer to having a noose slipped around his worthless neck. That thought pleasured me some.

Then I got to wondering again about the others, how come they was all so all-fired anxious to get their ass out to Denver. I couldn't believe none of their stories. There had to be something else. I wondered especial what that damn preacher could be running from, but I was curious too about the others, old Pelty and them two Purdy women. And then, looking at them women, which I done ever' now and then, I got to thinking about my old Lillian and about Bonnie Boodle too, and then I was wondering just what the hell was going on back home in Asininity.

I couldn't help thinking about that time I found Lillian all wrapped around old Texas Jack what I had killed because of it, and now I had left her in Asininity with her own home and her own snitty supper club and plenty of cash and no one to watch out for my interests at all. Could be she might take a liking to someone. I recalled the way she had fluttered so sweet around old Happy back there when she had first seen that he was back. She might just go for old Happy, and if she was to go for him, wouldn't nothing stop her a-getting him.

I guess you done figgered out that it had been some time since I was real what you call in love with Lillian. Even so, she was my wife and the mother of my snot-nosed kid, and it kind of irked me, you might say, to think that she might be playing a tune with old Happy's fiddlestick while I was out there in the middle of nowhere getting my ass bounced around and shot at and such. 'Course, I had my own good times outside of the marriage bed with my old sweetie Bonnie Boodle, but then Bonnie had just recent bedded old Happy too.

Goddamn it, I thought. Could that little runt be right now as I'm riding into all this trouble a-screwing both my women? Damn his double-crossing hide, I said to myself. How could he do that to me? And after all I done for him, too. Hell, I give him a job. I got him his first taste of tail. I've bought him a lot of whiskey, too. I been like his poppa and his big brother and a damn good friend. And he would jump both my women when I'm out of town?

I built him up to old Peester, our mayor, too. I even kind of lied about him. I said he'd had experience. Well, technical he had been my deputy once, but all I had him to do was to just set on a stool in the Hooch House with a shotgun and keep an eye out for any trouble that might develop in there. I had made him a deputy so the town would pay his salary 'stead of me having to do it. That's all the deputy he ever was. Now I had him acting in my own marshaling position while I was away. I begun to wonder again if I had made a fool move in taking this trip. I could have sent Happy 'stead of me.

Well hell, it was really too late for that kind of thinking, so I turned my meanness on poor old Jug Marlin. "Hey, Jug," I said, "what you thinking about?" He looked at me, but he didn't say nothing. "You still thinking that there brother of yours is going to get you out of this mess you're in?" He give me a hard look on that one, but he still kept quiet. "You beginning to think about how heavy your ass end is? Say, Jug, anyone ever tell you the story 'bout what happened whenever they hanged old Black Jack Ketchum? You heard that one?"

"I heard it," he said, but I just ignored him.

"Well," I said, "it seems as how old Black Jack had gained some weight while he was locked up, you know. He was just setting there in that cell a-waiting to hang. He wasn't riding no horse a-running from the law or chasing trains to rob or nothing. So he just natural put on some extra pounds, you know. Now, these goddamn hangmen, they don't always know what the hell they're doing. You know, Jug, there's damn few experts out there anymore. Anyone can get a job doing just about any damn thing. It's a sin and a shame. You know, for instance, anyone can say he's a preacher and then just go to it."

"A man must have the calling from God," Harp said.

"This here's a private conversation, Preacher," I said. "Mind your business. Don't pay no attention to him, Jug. Hell, he'll be wanting to pray over you. But

111

getting back to old Black Jack. He had put on considerable weight, it seems, so the day come when they had him set to hang, and they tied his hands behind his back, you know, and they tuck him out of the cell and marched him out in the yard where they had built a brand-new scaffold just for the occasion and they marched him up them steps to the platform and stood him on that trapdoor. Then they put a black sack over his head."

"I don't want to hear this, Barjack," Jug said.

"Barjack," the preacher snapped at me, "that's quite enough."

"The hangman, incompetent as he was, put the noose around old Black Jack's head," I went on, ignoring the both of them, "but the damn fool left way too much slack in the rope, you see. Well, when they final dropped old Black Jack, they never really hanged him at all. What with all that slack and all the extra weight he had put on, what they actual done was, they just snapped his head off. Snapped it right off."

"Ugh," said Van Pelt.

"How awful," said old lady Purdy, and the young Purdy just kind of shivered.

"You're inhumane, Barjack," said Harp. "Inhumane and un-Christian and totally uncalled for."

"And you're an asshole," I said to him.

"I'm going to be sick," Jug said.

"Well, stick your damn head out the window," I said. "Don't be puking in here."

Of a sudden, I felt the coach slow down and heard old Goose Neck call out, "Whoa. Whoa up there.

Whoa now." We come to a fast rocking stop, and I opened the door and stepped out, looking up at Goose Neck.

"What the hell?" I said.

"Look ahead," said Goose Neck, and so I did, and then I seen what had stopped him. The road ahead was piled up with rocks. Big ones and little ones and a whole bunch in between. I tuck a quick gander up the side of the hill, and I could see that it was the result of a recent slide.

"Goddamn it," I said.

Goose Neck yelled out, "Everyone out." Just then I seen a figure raise up from behind all them rocks. He was holding a rifle, and he had a serious look on his ugly face. I stayed behind the open door.

"You're in range of this scattergun," I heard Ash Face say. Real easy, I reached inside the coach for my Winchester, and I cranked a shell into the chamber.

"I'm Hooper," the man behind the rocks said. "All I want is Jug."

"Orvel?" said Jug Marlin, kind of perking up.

"Shut up," I said.

"Barjack," said Goose Neck, "you talk to him."

I stepped out from behind the open door then and tuck me a good look at Orvel Hooper, the last survivor of the four would-be rescuers. "Orvel Hooper," I said.

"That's me," he said. "Who're you?" I told him, "I'm Marshal Barjack, and the man you're a wanting is my prisoner. I have orders to fetch him over to the marshal in Denver, and I mean to do it."

113

"I mean to stop you," Hooper said.

"Or die a-trying?" I asked him.

"That's a better choice than going back to Snake Eyes and telling him I didn't bring his brother back with me," Hooper said. "You got a rifle, and that old fart on top has a shotgun. One of you might get me, but I bet I can get one of you before I fall. Why not just give me Jug? I'll take him and ride on out of here. That's all. No one'll get hurt."

"You've done pissed me off, Hooper," I said. "We'll be working the rest of the day to clear off this road. Now, I've got a proposal for you. You toss me your guns and get to clearing away them rocks, and I won't even bother putting you under arrest. I'll just go on and turn old Jug in and not give you another thought. If you're so damn scared of old Snake Eyes, why, just mount up and ride east or south or north. You got three ways to choose from. You ain't got to go back to No Name."

"I'd be hiding the rest of my natural life," he said. "It ain't worth it. Now, I'm tired of talking. You going to give me Jug or not?"

I cradled my Winchester in the crook of my left arm and pulled out one of my Colts, which I cocked and aimed at old Jug's head. "Not alive, I ain't," I said.

Just then old Harp jumped out the far door and yelled, "Barjack, give him up."

Well, them might've been the words old Hooper wanted to hear, but he sure wasn't expecting to hear them from that source. Old Harp kind of startled him. He swung his rifle over in that direction, and when he did, I swung my Colt around and shot Hooper. I seen blood fly from his right shoulder where I nicked him. He yelled and turned on me again, but before he could take aim and squeeze, Ash Face cut loose. My God, that shotgun made a mess.

I looked over at Jug, and he looked like he wanted to cry. "My brother will kill you, Barjack," he said.

"That's what you told me these four was going to do," I said. "They're the ones that's dead, ain't they?"

Goose Neck started down off the box. "Let's clear the road, folks," he said.

Ever'one piled out, and I even made poor old Jug help by using his one good arm as best he could. Harp just stood there for a minute.

"Is the way safe now?" he said.

"I reckon it is, Preacher," I said. "By the way, I ought to thank you for what you done." He give me a real peculiar look.

"What do you mean?" he said.

"Why, me and old Ash Face there," I said, "we'd a never been able to blow old Hooper away like we done if you hadn't distracted him the way you done."

'Course, I knowed that he hadn't done that a purpose, and I knowed that he sure didn't mean to help us kill old Hooper. I was just gigging him a little for the fun of it. He huffed up, but for once he didn't seem to have no answer.

Ash Face heaved up a big rock and throwed it aside. He looked back over his shoulder at the rest of us and said, "Come on. Pitch in here." I went on over to help do my part, and so did the preacher. Even the two ladies begun to help. I noticed that Van Pelt was holding back, clutching that little bag to his chest.

"Get your ass over here and help, Pelty," I said.

"I—I . . ."

"Come on, by God," I said, and he come over kind of tentative-like, and he tuck hold of that goddamned little bag by its handle, holding it in his left hand, and with his right he picked up a little rock and throwed it off to the right side of the road. "You silly little bastard," I said, and I grabbed that bag of his out of his hand and tossed it out of the way.

"No," he yelled, and he started to go after it, but I grabbed him by his both shoulders and spun him around and shoved him right down on that big pile of rocks.

"Now, get to work like the rest of us," I said. Well, he did, but he wasn't happy about it, and he kept looking back over his shoulder to make sure that little bag was still setting there unmolested. Of a sudden, I was mighty curious about the contents of that little bag.

Chapter Nine

I thought them goddamn rocks was going to break my back before we ever got the road clear enough to drive on through, but final we had it damn near done. I had just tuck hold of the feet of the corpse to drag it off to the side, and there was one fair-sized boulder left in the way. Ash Face put his shoulder to it and looked around. The preacher had his hands full of a rock and was staggering over to the side of the road with it. Goose Neck and Jug, of course, was both hurt. Van Pelt had just throwed a small rock, so Ash Face turned on him. "Give me a hand here," he said. Pelty looked like he'd really rather not, but after I had shoved him the way I done, I guess he figured that he'd better. He laid into that big boulder with Ash Face, and they got to moving it all right.

That give me the chance I was looking for. I

dropped the feet of the stiff and left it laying there beside the road. Then I walked over to Van Pelt's bag, laying there where I had tossed it earlier, and I picked it up. Whenever old Pelty and Ash Face had got that last big rock out of the way, Pelty turned around real desperate-like, looking for his bag. He seen that I had it, and he come a-running. He jerked it out of my hands, and he looked real furious for such a wimpy little guy. "Give me that," he said.

"Why, that's all I was fixing to do," I said. It come into my head that he was awful protective of a bunch of bank papers.

Ash Face had turned around and set down on that big boulder him and Pelty had pushed, and he was breathing hard and mopping his brow with an old red bandanna. I tuck out my flask and had me a short drink. Then all the rest of us looked around for a place to set and breathe. I set down on a rock near where old Jug had collapsed. "Well," I said, "that was the last of them. Four men come riding out to save your ass, and four men is dead."

"Snake Eyes is waiting at No Name," he said, "but you'll never even get there. He'll send out some more. He's got six more men. He'll send them out for me."

"Well, let's consider that possibility," I said. "Old Snake Eyes is wanted by ever' lawman in the West. It seems to me that if he's got six men setting around him, he ain't about to send them out to save your ass and stay behind all by his lonesome and unguarded. So even if you're right, and they try again, Snake Eyes most likely will come along with them. We done tuck care of four, and you told me they was all good men. Six ain't so much more than four. We'll deal with them all right."

"He won't ride out of No Name," said Jug. "He'll wait for you there. You won't know where they are. You won't know them when you see them. They'll pick you off like a setting goose."

"Well," I said, "I reckon we'll just see about that."

I got up and walked ahead just a little. I knowed that there had to be a horse tied up somewheres just off the road, and soon enough I found it. I led it back to the back end of the stagecoach and tied it there alongside the other one. I had me an idea about how to get around No Name without having to deal with old Snake Eyes and them other six men, but I figured I'd just keep my thoughts to myself for a spell.

Goose Neck didn't look as how he'd full recovered from all that road work, but I guess he figgered he couldn't afford to waste no more time. He stood up and hollered for us to all get loaded back into that coach, and so we did. We was a rough-looking bunch by then, I can tell you. Even them two Purdy ladies was all smudged with dirt. The young one's dress was tore, and they both had several wild strands of hair hanging down in their faces. We was going to make a real sight whenever we rolled into that next stop. And the next stop we would come to was one of them home stations. Goose Neck had done told us that we'd stop there for the night. We'd have us a supper and a floor to sleep on for the night. Then we'd have breakfast and get back on the road.

I figgered I could relax some and sip me some whiskey, so I pulled out my flask. I didn't figger on seeing no more outlaws that day nor for the rest of the night. Actual, what I figgered was that it would be the way me and Jug had spoke about. Snake Eyes and them other six would just wait around for us to roll on into No Name, and then they would try to take old Jug away from me there. When I really put my whole mind to it, I figgered that there wasn't no way he could know that we had done killed them first four he sent out, so there wouldn't be no reason for him to send out no more nohow. I tuck myself a good long drink, and I seen old Jug licking his lips again. I told him if he was thirsty, he could have some water.

"I'll be so glad when we reach the station tonight," the young Purdy said. "A bath and a change of clothes will do wonders for me."

"You won't find no bath there," I told her. "The best you're likely to find is a bowl of water and a rag. Maybe you can find a spot where you can hide yourself long enough to kind of wipe yourself off that way and then get your clothes changed."

She kind of blushed, and then the old lady said, "Well, if that's the way it is, then we'll just make do."

I wondered again about them two. Just what the hell was they running from or running to? Two fine ladies like that. 'Course, being dressed nice and smelling of perfume and acting like they done didn't fool me none. I had already been fooled by the best, and she had fooled my ass right into a wedding that I would never ever get over for the rest of my natural life. Hell, I thought, them two Purdy women could be high-class whores, for all I knowed. The old one had a wad of cash in her purse for sure. She had to of got it somewhere, and I suspected that she had not come by it honest. I tuck another good long drink, and then I begun to think that I should ought to have refilled my flask while we had been stopped back there.

"I for one," old Harp intoned, "will thank the Lord when this wretched trip is over at last."

"I'll feel greatly relieved myself," Pelty said.

"I reckon you will," I said. "I bet your arms are real tired from clutching that little bag so tight."

"It's been a long and tiring journey," old lady Purdy said. "I'm sure we'll all be glad to see the end of it."

"Old Jug here won't," I said, " 'cause the end of it for Jug is going to be a hanging, and it'll be his own neck what gets stretched."

"No, it won't," Jug said. "The end of the trip for you will be at No Name when my brother puts a bullet between your nasty little eyes."

"Miz Purdy, ma'am," I said to the old lady, "do you think I have nasty little eyes?"

"Why, I—"

"That's all right," I said. "You don't need to bother answering that question. Hell, I don't take any insults that old Jug here slings at me for serious."

"I'm afraid, Marshal," said Harp, "that you don't take anything seriously, and that includes the state of your own immortal soul."

"Tell me about that again, Preacher," I said. "About the state of my immortal soul. I been worrying some about it ever since you brought it up. Hell, I got to worry about it. If old Jug here is right, his brother is

121

going to blast me straight to hell as soon as we hit No Name."

"If I believed that you were serious, Marshal," Harp said, "I could tell you—"

"I ain't never been more serious," I said. "Wasn't you listening? I'm likely to be dead before this here stage ever reaches Denver."

"Unless you repent of your sins and beg forgiveness of the Lord in the name of his son and your savior Jesus Christ," Harp said, "your soul will be dragged screaming into the depths of hell, where it will be thrown into fire and brimstone and roast for all of eternity. There will be no rest and no relief. You will yearn for a cool breeze or a drink of water, but there will be none. You will cry and beg for oblivion, but it will not come. There will be nothing in your future, which will be forever and ever, except constant torture, and the pain and agony will be such that you will think that you cannot bear it, but bear it you must, for there will be no relief and no end to it."

"But if I repent?" I said.

"That is the first step," Harp said. He tuck on a real intense look then, and he was leaning over toward me real eager-like. "Do you truly repent of your sins?"

"I do," I said. "I really and truly do. I done fighting and killing and drinking and whoring, and I talked the worst kind of talk you ever heard, and I do truly repent me of all them wicked ways."

"And are you ready now to accept Jesus Christ, the son of the living God, as your only savior?" the preacher said. "Are you ready and willing to be transformed and reborn and to live forever in Christ?"

"I'm willing, Preacher," I said. "I'm willing."

"Take off your hat and bow your head," he demanded, and I done it, and he put a hand on top of my head. "O Holy God," he roared out, "we have witnessed here in these rude surroundings the miraculous conversion of a heathen of the worst kind into a lamb of your flock. This man Barjack, your humble servant, has truly repented of his sins before the world and has placed himself at the foot of your altar to beg your forgiveness for the wicked ways of his life. We plead with you, O Lord, to take this wretched sinner to your bosom and to receive into heaven his eternal soul. In the name of Christ Jesus we pray, Amen."

Old Miz Purdy said amen with him, and then the preacher tuck up a water jug and uncorked it, and he poured some water into the palm of his hand, and then he splashed the top of my head with it. "Is it done?" I said.

"It is," he said, and I looked up at him, and he had a real sweet smile on his ugly old face. I leaned back again.

"Well," I said, "that's some relief. I sure wasn't looking forward to that there brimstone."

"When you've truly given yourself to the Lord," Harp said, "the Lord will take care of you."

"Will he smite my enemies?" I asked.

"Yea, indeed," he said.

I looked over at Jug then, and I said, "What do you think about that, Jug? Your old snake-eyed brother is going to get hisself smote by the Lord. I ain't even got to worry about it no more."

"That's bull—," Jug said, and I slapped him across the face.

"Don't be spouting none of that kind of talk in front of the preacher," I said.

"Violence is unnecessary, Brother Barjack," said Harp. "The Lord will take care of Mr. Marlin for his sins."

"He will, huh?" I said. "You mean old Jug here is going to go down to all that there brimstone?"

"Unless he repent before he die," Harp said.

"You want to repent?" I asked Jug.

"You go to hell," Jug said.

"I'm afraid that's where you're bound, Jug," I said. Then I said, "Preacher, there's one thing still a-worrying me."

"What is it, Brother Barjack?" he said.

"Well," I said, "I ain't never been what you might call a real reader of the Bible."

"There's no time like the present," Harp said, and he dug one of them little black books right out of his pocket and handed it right over to me. I flipped through the pages some.

"Like I said," I went on, "I ain't never been much of a reader, but a feller showed me something in the good book once."

"Yes?" said old Harp.

"Well, what he showed me," I said, "it went something like this here. It said something like, 'I will cut off from old Jeroboam him what pisseth against the wall.' That there's what he showed me, and I pissed against a wall more than once in my life, so I'm wondering if I done been cut off or not, and if I ain't been, will I get cut off later on down the line, and when that happens is it going to render my recent baptism by yourself right here in this stagecoach and in front of these here witnesses useless as hell, or what?"

"You," Harp growled through clenched teeth. "You lied to me. You said all of that about repenting just to set me up for a dirty joke. You even caused me to perform a holy rite for the purpose of your own vile comic opera. You attempted to make a fool of me in front of witnesses. But the joke is on you, Barjack, and you won't find it to be very funny in the end."

I looked at the others in the coach, and then I said, "I think I just been cut off."

Van Pelt and the Purdy women just looked away from me, but old Jug in spite of hisself burst out laughing. I tuck myself another long drink, and then I thought about it for just a minute, and I handed the flask on over to old Jug. He tuck it, and he looked at me with surprise. He seemed like he didn't really know whether to believe me or not. "Go ahead," I said. After all, he was the only one in the coach who had appreciated what I had just did to old Harp. He tipped that flask up and tuck hisself a long drink, and I just let him. When he handed the flask back to me, it was empty. Lucky we rolled on into the home station just a little ways after that.

After we pulled in and stopped and quit rocking so violent, we all crawled out of the coach and went to unloading our bags. I didn't want nothing out of mine but just only one of my bottles that was stashed there. I didn't bother refilling my flask just then. I tuck it and the bottle along with me into the station. Being a home station, it was somewhat roomier than them swing stops, but still it wasn't nothing fancy. It did have a wood floor, though, 'cause that's where the company meant for us passengers to bed down. They had a stack of blankets for us to pick from.

Them two ladies found theirselves a little room in back where they tuck their bags and a bowl of water. After a while they come back out, and they looked all fresh and pretty again. They had also daubed on a bunch more of that strong-smelling perfume. It hit me like a wall as soon as they come out of that room. I let old Jug have another drink of whiskey, and he asked me if he could go out back. I followed him out there and checked the outhouse first, just in case. There wasn't no weapon in there, so I let him go, but only after I had made use of the place for myself.

Back inside, the station folks had laid out a real fine meal for us on a long plank table, and we all set down to eat. I stuffed myself full like a damn goose ready to be roasted, and then, 'cause I didn't really care for most of the company inside, I picked up a couple of blankets and tuck hold of old Jug and hauled his ass outside. "Where we going, Barjack?" he said.

"Come on along" was all I told him. Outside I looked around a bit and then decided that the coziest spot was over by the coach. The horses had all been put in the corral for the night, and so the coach was just setting there. I tossed them blankets down and told Jug to help me spread them out. He did, and then I said, "Set." He set down on one, and I set down on the other one. Then I uncorked that bottle. "We're going to get our ass drunk," I said.

Old Jug grinned real wide, and soon as I had tuck me a long swig, I handed him the bottle. He had hisself a healthy swig, and I could see right then that he was genuine appreciative. I also realized at that same time that I had actual tuck a liking to old Jug. That didn't make no sense to me till I got to thinking about how I was stuck on that damn stagecoach with all them other hypocritical assholes. Under the circumstances, I guessed, Jug was just about the best company.

'Course, Goose Neck and Ash Face was both okay, but they was on top all the time while I was stuck inside, and whenever we stopped, why, they was both kept pretty busy with their official duties and such. So they wasn't really much company.

"Barjack," Jug said, and I kind of snapped back out of my deep thoughts.

"What?" I said.

"Maybe I can talk my brother out of killing you," he said. "That is, if you let me go when we get to No Name."

"What about them four dead men along the trail?" I said. "Don't you reckon he'll want to take out some revenge on me for them?"

"We could tell him that old Ash Face done them all," Jug said. "Or that Longstreet. If I was to tell him that, he'd believe me. And I won't tell him that other stuff, you know, how you banged my head on the bars of your jail and starved me nigh to death and shot me in the shoulder."

"How is your shoulder?" I asked him.

"It's feeling some better," he said. "It still throbs, you know, and it hurts, but not near what it was."

"You ought to get it looked at by a real doc soon as you can manage it," I said.

"Well," he said, "what do you say?"

" 'Bout what?" I said.

" 'Bout telling Snake Eyes that you didn't kill none of them boys," he said. "Hell, Barjack, I don't want to see him kill you. I did for a while, but I don't no more. You ain't so bad."

I handed the bottle back to him, and he tuck another long drink. He give it back to me and looked kind of like apologetic, you know. "Looks like I damn near drank it all up," he said. I tilted it back and finished it. Then I tossed the bottle aside.

"There's more," I said. I struggled up onto my feet and around behind the coach, where I pulled another bottle out of my valise. I uncorked it and staggered back to my blanket. Handing the fresh bottle to Jug, I fell down on my spot. What I done was I started to set, but then I really kind of fell. Soon as I steadied myself up, Jug handed me the bottle and I tuck a drink.

"You sore all over?" I asked him.

"Yeah," he said. "I am, sure enough. Them goddamned rocks."

"Hell," I said, "it was your buddy Hooper what caused us to have to do that."

"I never liked old Hooper all that much nohow," Jug said. I passed the bottle to him, and he sucked on it.

"I'm just as glad to hear that," I said, " 'cause he's sure enough dead as hell."

"Speaking of hell," Jug said, "I sure did like the way you cut that damn preacher down to size. I thought I wasn't never going to be able to stop laughing. Did you see his face? Looked like he was about to bust several blood vessels, didn't it?"

"I don't want to cause the preacher to have no stroke," I said. "That might put me in even deeper brimstone."

At that, Jug commenced to laughing hard at the preacher again, and we had us a few more drinks, and pretty soon he passed out. I was kind of sorry about that, 'cause that left me to drink on alone, and I did that for a while longer. Then I figgered I might ought to get myself some sleep, but just as I was about to snuggle myself down for the night, I heard some footsteps.

Chapter Ten

I hauled out one of my trusty Colts, ready for damn near anything except what I seen. By God if it weren't the old lady Purdy. She come right up to the coach, and she kind of squatted down and peered underneath where I was a-laying on my blanket. Old Marlin was out from underneath, but I was kinda stuck mostly under. She was on the other side, but she squatted down and bent her head over to look under there and see me. 'Course it was dark, and she couldn't be sure what she was looking at. "Mr. Barjack," she said, and she kept her voice kinda low. "Mr. Barjack, is that you under there?"

Whenever I shuck off my initial surprise at who it was come looking for me, I said, "Yes, ma'am. It sure as hell is me under here."

"Mr. Barjack," she said, "I'd like to talk to you."

"Well, ma'am," I said, "I'm done bedded down here for the night."

"Would it be all right, then," she said, "if I just crawled under there to join you for a while?"

"To talk?" I said.

"Yes," she said. "To talk."

"Well," I said, "if you're a mind to, I reckon I won't object none. 'Course, if anyone was to see you under here with me, they might conjure up some wild ideas, if you get my meaning."

"I get your meaning, Mr. Barjack," she said, and she was already down on her hands and knees and crawling underneath. "I can deal with the gossip-mongers if need be."

Well, I kind of liked her for taking it that way, and when she come closer, I noticed her sweet perfume, and somehow it wasn't near as overwhelming as it had been before. It was kind a nice, you know, and even though it was dark, when she come close to me, I really seen her up close and real good for the first time. And you know what? For an old gal, she was a damn good looker. She for real was. A little plump, I guess, but what the hell. I had been happy and content with old Bonnie Boodle and her broad ass and bouncing tits for a good long while, clean up till I run onto that beautiful Lillian. Then I married Lillian and got used to her, and damned if I hadn't gone back to old Bonnie, at least part time. So Miz Purdy, she didn't really look half bad when I final tuck me a good look at her.

She crawled on over real close, and then she set down on her rump, but she was real hunkered over, 'cause if she hadn't a been her head would a been knocking against the bottom of the coach. "I can't sit like this," she said. "Do you mind?" And she slickered herself down till she was laying right snug beside me. I couldn't hardly believe what I thought was happening, and I hoped that I hadn't drunk myself too damn much whiskey to be able to do proper work whenever the right time come for it.

"Well," I said, deciding to take it slow and easy, "what's on your mind, ma'am?"

Then she said, "First of all, Mr. Barjack, please call me Idabelle."

"Just Idabelle?" I said.

"Yes," she said, "just Idabelle."

"Well, all right, Idabelle," I said, "I'll do that, if you'll drop the mister and just call me Barjack."

"All right," she said, and damned if she didn't snuggle over against me. "There's a chill in the night air," she said, and so I scooted myself some against her and agreed that it was so. It was only then, feeling her body press up against mine, that I realized that she wasn't dressed no more. I don't mean that she was nekkid, but what she was wearing was one of them long flannel nightgowns, you know, and I figured that likely she didn't have nothing on underneath it. I was aiming to find out pretty soon, too.

"Idabelle," I said, "a little snort of good whiskey does wonders on a cool night like this."

"I couldn't agree more, Barjack," she said.

'Course right then I uncorked that bottle and handed it to her, and damned if she didn't turn it up and gulp down a healthy snort. I told you before that

I wasn't fooled no more by them fancy women. Not since Lillian. She handed the bottle back to me, and I tuck another snort. I didn't really want it, but I didn't think it would look right, me giving her a snort and then not taking one myself. I jobbed the cork back in and set the bottle aside. Then I scooched my face on up close to the side of her head, and I said, "What was it you wanted to talk to me about, Idabelle?"

"I wanted to ask you," she said, "if you think that we're really in any danger."

"Naw," I said, acting real tough, "I don't believe that you are. Not now. I reckon I could still be in some danger, but I think the rest of you're going to be just as safe as if you was at home."

"When you say that, Barjack," she said, "I believe you. I feel much better already." With that she turned her face to mine, and she pressed her lips to mine, and we had us one of them lingering sloppy kisses, you know, and I forgot all about that young one inside, and all about Bonnie Boodle and all about Lillian by God Mrs. Barjack.

Well, I swear, it wasn't no time before she tackled my belt buckle and the fly fastenings of my britches and had pulled it all down to my knees. I didn't need much encouraging, neither, before I was full ready for her. Then she hiked up that flannel nightshirt she was wearing and just clumb on top of me like as if I was a wild bronc, and by God that's what she made me feel like too, and it tuck her a while, but by God she broke me. She plumb broke me. Damn, but she was a bronc-riding old bitch. Then she give me a peck on the cheek and away she went. I just laid there feeling somewhat stunned by the whole experience. I thought briefly about Lillian and Bonnie and Happy and ever'body and ever'thing back at Asininity, and I thought to myself that I for real had broke loose from all that. It felt good.

I didn't really feel like going right to sleep after that riding I got, so I uncorked that bottle again, and before I got myself real drowsy, I had emptied the son of a bitch. Then I final dropped off, either by just going to sleep or by passing out. I ain't real for sure which. But the next thing I knowed someone was hollering around, and I woke up, and the sun was a-coming out low in the east. I moaned and groaned and crawled out from under that stagecoach before I realized that my britches was still down around my knees. Well, I hauled them up real quick-like and looked around to see if anyone was a watching, but I didn't see no one. I fastened them up, and then I was for sure wide awake. I kicked old Jug and hollered at him to come around, and then I headed for the outhouse.

By the time I got myself inside the station, the coffee was hot and the breakfast was being laid out on the table. Jug was a-setting at the table, and when he seen me, he said, "I brought the blankets back in, Barjack." He was acting like he was a schoolkid and I was the teacher and he had done good. I just give him a nod and then set myself down right by him. "We had us a good one last night, didn't we, Barjack?" he said.

I looked across the table at old Idabelle, and then I said, "Yeah, Jug, we sure enough did."

Idabelle said, "Good morning, Mr. Barjack," and I caught on right quick, and I said, "Morning, ma'am." From then on, she didn't act no different to me than she had before our rodeo ride of the night before. What a hell of a woman she was, I reckon.

"How soon will we be under way?" piped up old Harp.

"What's your hurry, Preacher?" I asked him. "The Devil a-chasing you?"

"The Devil chases all men, Marshal," he said. "He caught up with you long ago, and he seems to have his claws locked firmly into your flesh. I fear you'll never escape."

"Well, hell," I said, "if he keeps on a giving me as much fun as I been having, I reckon we'll get along together in hell all right, me and him. You ought to slow down a bit and let him catch up with you. You'd find out he ain't such a bad feller after all." When I said that, I seen old Idabelle give me a little look, but when I looked back at her that look had done vanished already and had been replaced by that snooty one she used in public.

Goose Neck stood up from the table and wiped his mouth with his sleeve. "Folks," he said, "I'm going on out now to hitch up a fresh team. Don't be rushing yourselfs, though. You've got plenty of time to eat all you want and have an extra cup or two of coffee before we board. When we're ready to go, I'll give a holler." Then he walked on out, and pretty soon Ash Face follered him.

"Mr. Barjack," Idabelle said, talking real formal-

135

like, "do I understand correctly that you believe the danger is over to the passengers?"

"Why, uh, yes, ma'am," I said, trying hard to be half as good as she was at that there playacting, "I do believe that. You see, old Snake Eyes, this here Jug's brother and the leader of that gang of outlaws, is a-waiting for me in No Name, and he don't want nothing from none of you. All he wants is to save old Jug here from the hangman. Well, he sent out them four, and we done killed all of them, but he don't know that. I reckon he'll just wait it out at No Name."

Shortly after that we all got loaded up again and was back out on the road. I had the foresight to refill my flask, and all of us passengers was back in the same seats we had occupied before. Pelty was a-hugging the little bag to his chest. The two Purdy women were setting up stiff with their noses in the air, and old Harp was scowling like the very devil was in the coach with him. Old Jug looked pretty damned relaxed and not really too unhappy. I wondered if that was 'cause he figured it wouldn't be too long before I was killed and he was set free. But somehow I didn't think that was really right. Somehow I didn't think that old Jug really wanted to see me killed no more, not like he done before. And I wasn't none too sure that I wanted to see him hang, neither.

Well, we was rambling along pretty good there when all of a sudden I was startled by the nearby sound of a shotgun blast. I can tell one all right, and that's what it was, and what's more, I didn't think that it had come from old Ash Face right up there on the box. It wasn't quite that close. Then I heard someone holler something that I couldn't quite make out, and I heard Goose Neck whoa them horses and felt him slowing down and then stopping the stage. We set there rocking, and I shushed all the others in there with me, while I slipped out one of my Colts and cocked it. I give old Jug a hard look, and he just kind a shrugged as if to say to me that he didn't know what the hell was going on. Then I heard a voice call out, "Drop that gun," and I thought I could tell the sound of old Ash Face's gun hitting the ground.

"Throw down that box," the voice said.

"We ain't carrying nothing but passengers on this run," Goose Neck said. "You've hit the wrong stage, friend."

"Ha," the road agent called out. "That's a good one, but I ain't falling for it. Climb down off a there. Both of you."

We could feel the motions from Goose Neck and Ash Face a-climbing down, and then I figured the next motions was when the road agent clumb up. "Goddamn it," I heard him say. Then he clumb on up on top of the coach, and he commenced to opening bags and then tossing them down on the ground. I figgered he must be looking for some loot in the bags. He cussed again and clumb down, and he made Goose Neck and Ash Face walk around back and open up the boot, and then I reckon he started in on the bags back there. I hoped that the son of a bitch would leave my whiskey alone. I was about to slip open the door and see if I couldn't move on around and get him while he was involved with the bags, but he stopped me.

"Damn it," I heard him say. "I reckon there's nothing for it but to rob all your passengers. Come on. Move over there to the side." So I knowed he was coming. I seen Goose Neck and Ash Face walk right past me, and then I seen him right close up. He was standing right by the door and looking in right at me through the window. I was holding my Colt down low, and he never seen that. He had a bandanna pulled up over his nose, so all I could see of him was his eyes, and they was cold blue. "Come on out of there," he said, and he grabbed the handle and pulled the door open, and soon as he done that I fired a round into his chest.

"Ah hell," he said, and he fell over backwards. Ash Face moved fast and picked up his shotgun. He didn't have no other weapon on him. I stepped on out and looked down at him. "You son of a bitch," he said, "you've done for me."

"I reckon that was my intention," I said. "Like the man told you, you picked the wrong stage."

"Goddamn it," he said. "I'm dying."

"It had to come sooner or later," I said. "You just rushed it along a little, that's all."

"You want a preacher, man?" Goose Neck asked him. "We got one on board."

"A preacher?" the man said. He lifted his hand up off his bloody chest and looked at it. "Yeah. Yeah, I do."

"Harp," I said, "come on out here. We got you a customer."

Harp come out of the coach a-toting his Bible, and

got down on one knee beside the dying man. "Brother," he said, "you're going to meet your maker. Do you repent of your sins?"

I didn't want to hear too much of that, but I did want something else to do with the bastard. I looked into the coach at old Jug, and I said, "Jug, get your ass out here." He clumb out. The mask had fell down off the road agent's face, and I pointed at him. "Who is it?" I said.

Jug said, "I ain't never seen him before, Barjack. I swear it. He ain't one of Snake Eyes's boys."

"Come on and give me a hand," I said. I led Jug around to the back of the stage where the bastard had rummaged through the bags there, mine included. There was opened bags and clothes throwed all over the road. Then I seen that one of my bottles had been broke. "Goddamn it," I roared. "The son of a bitch has wasted a bottle of good whiskey. If he ain't for real dying, I will kill him now."

Jug picked up another bottle. "This one didn't break, Barjack," he said. We picked up all my stuff, including the one bottle, and put it back into my valise. Then I fastened my valise up again and tossed it back into the boot. The others had got out by then and was gathering up their own things. I walked around to the front end where Ash Face was standing and holding two shotguns. He had picked up his own and the one the owlhoot had been using.

"I don't know how I let that bastard get the drop on me, Barjack," he said. "It ain't never happened before. Hell, maybe I'm just getting old."

"Ah," I said, "there's a first time for ever'thing,

Ash Face. Don't let it worry you none. Just don't let it happen again."

"The good thing is that no one got hurt," said Goose Neck, just coming around to join us. "Nothing got stole from us neither."

"I lost a good bottle of whiskey," I said.

"It was my fault," said Ash Face. "I'll buy you one to replace it soon as we get to No Name."

"Well," I said, "I just hope I'll be alive to collect it."

Then I heard the road agent gurgle and gag, and then he was quiet. We all walked around to the other side, and Harp looked up at us and said, "He's gone to meet his maker." I walked on over and tucked the toe of my boot underneath the corpse and give it a shove to roll it off the road. Harp come up to his feet. "Barjack," he said, "have you no respect for the dead?"

"We can't leave him lay in the road," I said, "and we ain't got no room for him on the stage. Unless you want to carry him in your lap."

Harp snorted and walked away, and Goose Neck said, "Let's get rolling. We still have a schedule to keep."

We all got back into our places, and Goose Neck started us rolling west again. I pulled out my flask and had myself a drink. Killing always seems to call for whiskey. I passed the flask on over to Jug, and he grinned his appreciation and helped hisself. "Mr. Barjack," Idabelle said, "you were wonderful."

"Why, thank you, ma'am," I said.

"He just killed a man," Harp said.

"Well," said Van Pelt, "I for one am very grateful," and I seen he was really holding tight to his little satchel.

"Reverend Harp," the young Miss Purdy said, "I hate to disagree with you, but for once I must. That man might have killed us all. At the very least, he would have robbed us. Mr. Barjack saved us all from that."

Well, old Harp couldn't hardly stand to listen to me being praised, but he didn't have nothing more to say. He just clamped his lips together real tight and frowned as hard as he could manage and stared straight ahead. Jug handed me back my flask, and I tuck myself another drink. I had a mind to offer it to Idabelle, but I knowed she was playing her old proper self again there in front of the others, so I never.

Nothing much happened all the way to the next two swing stops, and then I knowed that we only had one more before we would be on the way into No Name and I would have to face old Snake Eyes and his gang. The closer we come to it, the more I thought on it. "Jug," I said, "how many men did you say old Snake Eyes has got left?"

"The best I can count," he said, "he's got six, and with him that makes seven. Barjack, you're good, but you can't fight seven."

"You wouldn't be lying to me, would you?" I asked him.

"No," he said. "Hell no, Barjack, I wouldn't lie to you. I would have once, but I won't no more. You been good to me lately. 'Course, you mean to turn me in to get hung, but then I guess it's just your job, and I really can't blame you none for that."

Well, I believed him. I ain't sure why, but I did. What's more, whenever he said what he said I got me a real soft feeling in my chest and gut, and it bothered me real bad. I knowed then that I didn't want to stick around and watch the show whenever they did string him up, and it was only then that I begun to think of the hanging as something for real. I hadn't done that before. I was just delivering a prisoner. That was all. Oh, I had knowed, all right, that they would most likely hang him, and I had even badgered him about it for a while, but I hadn't really thought of it as a for-real sure thing. And a course, I hadn't really got to know old Jug yet back then, neither.

Chapter Eleven

Well, final come the night that we unloaded ourselfs at the last home station before No Name. The ladies washed theirselves up again and got theirselves ready for a night of sleep on the floor. I figgered that I'd bed down outside under the coach again just in case the old lady got herself another itch and was to want me to scratch it for her again. I wasn't ready to bed down just yet, though, 'cause I knowed that the next day we'd be going on into No Name, and I might could be dead before that night. So I figgered that if this here was to be my last night on earth, well, I wanted it to be a good one. I figgered on getting blind drunk with old Jug. He had turned out to be a good drinking partner, all right.

So I fetched us a couple of chairs up to a table there inside the station, and we commenced to drinking real serious. We'd had us a couple of good tumblers full before either one of us said anything that amounted to much, but then old Jug looked me right smack in the eyeballs, and he said, "Barjack, goddamn it, I sure do hate to think about old Snake Eyes shooting you dead when we get on into No Name. Hell, I've actual come to like you."

"That was a right kind thing for you to say," I told him. "And since you done said it, I'll just go on ahead and tell you that I sure ain't looking forward to your hanging none too much neither."

Old Jug he kind of shook his head at that, and then he looked at me again, and he said, "Barjack, ain't you figgered out yet that there ain't going to be no hanging? You ain't going to get me to Denver to turn me in. You ain't going to get out of No Name alive. There just ain't no way you can take on Snake Eyes and them other six men and come out alive. God, I hate see it happen. If you was to let me talk to him, Barjack, maybe I could talk him out of killing you."

"That would mean I'd have to let you go, wouldn't it?" I said.

"Well," he said, and he scratched his head, "yeah. I guess it would at that." And then he kind of grinned.

"I ain't going to do it," I said. "I can't. It's my duty to turn you over in Denver. Hell, the reward's done been paid. It's been paid by my town, and before I can get it paid back to my town, I got to turn you in. You see?"

Jug tuck hisself another drink, and then he said, "How much was the reward?"

"Five hundred bucks," I said.

"What if I could get my brother to pay you back the five hundred?" he said.

"Jug," I said, and I said it like as if I was real exasperated with him, "Jug, I'm a goddamned lawman, and what you're doing is offering me a bribe. Just get drunk. Have fun." But the truth is I was contemplating the offer he had just made me. You see, I didn't really want old Jug to get his neck stretched. Not no more. But even more important, I didn't want to see old Snake Eyes kill me dead neither."

Jug said he had to go out to piss, and I told him to just go on ahead. "Well," he said, "what if I was to run off?"

"You ain't going to run off," I said. "It's a long walk on over to No Name from here, and you're a lazy son of a bitch. Go on."

Well, he got up and walked over to the door, and I wasn't really paying too much attention. I seen old Aunt Idabelle come out of the back room, and she was wearing that there nightie thing again. I was recalling just how her legs and ass felt underneath it, and I didn't know if she had that old itch again, but I was beginning to feel a powerful urge myself. But even though I wasn't paying no real attention to old Jug, I seen him out of the corner of my eye when he opened the door and then shut it again right quick. He come hurrying back over to where I was setting, and then I paid some more attention to him.

"What the hell's wrong with you?" I said.

"I just seen Butch ride up," he said.

"Who the hell's Butch?" I asked him.

"Butch Banner," he said. "He's one of Snake

Eyes's boys. He'll be coming through that door now in just a minute, Barjack."

I tried to jump up and pull out my right-hand Colt at the same time, but I forgot to shove my chair back. I got the Colt out, but when I went to bring it up into position, I hit my hand on the underside of the table-top. The Colt went off, and I sent a shot into the floor. The shot was loud as hell in that closed room, and the ladies screamed. Harp and Van Pelt both went underneath tables. I fell back in my chair so hard that I turned it over. My knees hit the table and tilted it up, and my bottle fell over, spilling good whiskey.

Well, I just natural scrambled to save the whiskey. I jerked that bottle up by its neck. I was still on my own knees, though, when I done it. The whiskey was almost up to the halfway mark, so I didn't lose too much of the good stuff, but just then the door got kicked open real hard, and that gunslick Butch jumped inside and over to his right, his back against the wall and a gun in each hand.

Jug was still standing there by the table, and he was between me and Butch. "Hold it, Butch," he said.

Butch yelled, "Get out of the way," and just then old Ash Face popped up from somewheres, and damned if he didn't cut loose with both barrels. Butch didn't even have time to yell. He was damn near cut in half, and blood was splattered all over the wall there behind him. He crumpled up in a bloody mess on the floor. I stood up then, Colt in my hand, and I strolled over to the body, looking as official as I knowed how.

"Reckon he's done for," I said. I glanced over my

shoulder at Jug and added, "He ride in alone, did he?"

"I didn't see no one else," he said.

"Well," I said, "let's drag him out of here, and then I reckon we ought to settle our ass down outside. We can keep a better watch that way. Just in case."

We done all that, and when I got our blankets laid out under the coach, old Jug, he didn't lay down. He just stood there looking kind of sheepish. "What's wrong?" I said.

"Barjack," he said, "I pissed my pants."

I told him to take them off and throw them away. I figgered that old Harp was about Jug's size, and whoever thought about a preacher without a extra pair of britches. I left Jug hiding under his blanket without no britches on, and I went back inside. I kept as quiet as I knowed how, and I found the preacher a-snoring away on the floor. His britches was hanging over a chair back right there beside him, so I tuck them.

They fit Jug all right. While he was pulling them on, I asked him, "You think you can ride horseback with that bum arm?"

"I reckon I can," he said. "What for?"

"Oh," I said, "it's just something I'm scheming on. Forget it and have a drink." I handed him the bottle I had brought out from the table, the one I had nearly spilled in my time of danger. He tuck hisself a good long drink and give it back to me. I was thinking of how I might could find a way to get my job done without having to face up to old Snake Eyes, but I wasn't right sure just how much I had ought to tell Jug.

I give him some more whiskey and slowed down

on it myself, and pretty soon my little trick worked. He had passed on out. I had me one more drink, then I got up and slipped back inside. I located Idabelle, but she was snoring like hell. I guess she didn't have no itch that night. I went on back out to my blanket, and I just set there for a spell thinking things over. You see, what I was thinking was that I could saddle up two horses early in the morning, take old Jug with me, and just ride wide around No Name. Snake Eyes would be looking for us to come into No Name on the stagecoach, and by the time he found out we wasn't there, why, we'd be halfway to Denver. I'd get Jug turned in and wouldn't have to fight no one nowhere along the way. Then I'd cash in my return ticket and go back to Asininity some other way.

That's what I was thinking, but there was something that wasn't setting quite right with me about it. I couldn't quite figger it out. Oh, I knowed, a course, that I didn't really want old Jug to hang, but I didn't think that was the thing that was troubling me about my scheme. I had done told myself and Jug too that I was going to have to do my duty and turn him in to that United States marshal, so my mind was made up. I wasn't having no struggle with them kind of thoughts at all. It was something else entire.

But when I had woke up in the early morning, it had all come to me. I knowed all at once what I was going to do. Since old Ash Face had blowed Butch apart the night before, I now had myself three outlaw horses. I got myself up while it was still dark and saddled up all three of them. I tuck my valise and tied it onto one saddle, and then I stole myself some blankets from the station, and I rolled old Butch up in them and tied the bundle up real good. I loaded him back onto his own saddle and tied him down right proper. By then the other folks was starting to stir, and I kicked old Jug awake. "Let's get us some eats," I said.

We went inside the station, and Preacher Harp was standing in there with his face as red as hell and a blanket wrapped around his legs. When he seen Jug, he pointed at him and yelled out, "There they are. Those are my trousers. Give them back, you thief."

Old Jug looked at me kind of helpless-like, and I said, "Preacher, I don't know what your problem is, but old Jug here is my prisoner. I been watching him real careful all night long, and if he had stole hisself a pair of britches, I'd know about it. That's for sure."

"They're mine, I tell you," Harp roared. "I left them right there on the chair overnight, and this morning they were gone, and he's wearing them. Take them off, and give them back to me this instant."

"Now, Preacher," I said, "it's too bad that your britches has disappeared, but as far as I can tell, one old pair of britches, special them plain black ones, looks pretty much like another pair. It ain't right, you accusing old Jug here. Hey, come to think on it, I seen what looked like a pair of britches a-laying out there in the yard. Maybe them's yours."

Well, he fussed some more, but there wasn't nothing he could do for it but final just hop on outside in his blanket to look for them britches I had told him about. I figgered that if he was lucky they might have dried some by then, and since they'd been laying outside all night, maybe the fresh air would have blowed most of the smell of piss out of them. If he was lucky.

We set down to eat, and by and by the preacher come back in a-wearing Jug's old britches, and I noticed right off that I had been wrong about the smell. He was mad, too. But then, it seemed to me that he was always mad, and I thought as how I was doing him a favor by giving him a good reason to be that-away. "These are not my trousers," he said, "and they're filthy."

I said, "Well, Preacher, whyn't you get out a fresh pair and change to them." He set down at the far end of the table keeping as much away from ever'one as he could, and he never answered my question. Then it come to me that he had been even in more of a hurry to get out of Asininity than I had been thinking. I recalled that I hadn't never seen no bag for him. He hadn't tuck time to pack no clothes.

I et up and hurried old Jug along, and I slipped as many biscuits as I could into my pockets before I left the table. Then I made sure that we had plenty of water and whiskey and I had all my guns loaded. I sidled up to old Ash Face, and I said to him real low, "Don't be surprised if me and old Jug ain't on the stage when it pulls out."

He said, "What's up, Barjack?"

"I'm taking Jug and riding wide around No Name," I said.

"Oh," Ash Face said. "I get it. Be careful, Barjack."

"That's just what I'm a doing," I said.

I tuck Jug on out and we mounted up. Goose Neck and the station man was just then getting out the new team in order to hitch them up. It was still dark. I was getting us out of there in real good time. "Come on," I said. We moved onto the road, me a-leading the third horse with the smelly load on its back. I kept us on the road till the sun come out and started in lighting things up from the east. Then I led the way out in the field and then farther on away from the road till we was well out where no one riding down the road would spot us out there. Then I headed us west again.

"Barjack," Jug said, "what are we doing?"

"You told me that I couldn't live through a fight with old Snake Eyes and them," I said. "So I'm taking your word for it, by God, and I'm avoiding a fight. We ain't going into No Name a'tall."

"You mean, we're riding horseback from here all the way into Denver?" he said.

"That's right," I told him, and I pulled a bottle out of the saddlebag where I had put it and handed it to him. He tuck a drink, and I reckon that he was beginning to think all of a sudden that he really would hang, and I would live on after all. What I didn't tell him was that there was more to my plan than just riding around No Name, but the thing was, I didn't rightly know just yet how I was going to pull off the rest of it, so I didn't say nothing about it to him.

"He'll figger it out, Barjack," Jug said. "He might not figger it out in time to save me, but he'll figger it out, and he'll be coming for you."

"We'll see," I said. Jug handed the bottle over to me, and I tuck myself a drink.

"Barjack," he said, "let me go."

"We done talked about that, Jug," I said.

"But what good's it going to do if both of us winds up dead?" he said. "Let me go, and we'll both stay alive."

"Shut up, Jug," I said.

We rode till the sun was high overhead, and then I pulled them biscuits out of my pocket, and we et them. We et them all, and that meant that we didn't have nothing more to eat. It looked to be a long ride to Denver. Then I seen an old jackrabbit, and I pulled out my Winchester and got him with one shot. We stopped and built us a fire and cooked that tough old thing. It wasn't much good, but it was better than going hungry. I improved the meal somewhat by pulling out the bottle, so we could wash that tough nasty meat down with good whiskey.

"Barjack," Jug said, but I didn't let him go on.

"I ain't turning you loose," I said.

I put out the fire, and we mounted up and continued along our way. Ever' now and then old Jug tried to talk me into turning him loose, but I either shut him up or just didn't pay no attention to him. I was scheming in my own mind on more important things. Then at last we had rode most of the day away. My stomach was complaining to me something fierce, and I was trying to calm down my hunger with whiskey. Jug was hungry too, and I was passing the bottle back and forth with him. Then by and by he said, "No Name's right over yonder." He pointed south.

"You mean we've rode even with it?" I asked him.

"If we'd been on the road," he said, "we'd a been there an hour or so ago."

I commenced to wondering if there might be some
way of riding into No Name and getting a good steak
dinner without running into old Snake Eyes, but I
couldn't come up with nothing. The sun was low, and
I wondered if maybe I could spot another four-legged
meal for us before it come full dark. I didn't see nothing, though. I decided that with dark coming on, we
might ought to go ahead and find a camp spot for the
night, and I said something about it to Jug.

"What're you going to do about old Butch?" he
said.

"What do you mean?" I said.

"Well," he said, "I don't hardly think I can sleep
with that stink."

Then it come on me what it was that had been
nagging at my brain and why I had brung that stinking
stiff along. What I could do, I could do all by my
lonesome, but I didn't much relish going through the
rest of my life a-looking back over my shoulder for
old Snake Eyes. I had to somehow get it cleared with
him. "Jug," I said, "if I was to let you go for a short
spell to do something, could I trust you to come
back?"

"What?" he said.

"I want you to give me your word that you'll come
back if I let you ride out by yourself," I said.

"Well, what is it you want me to do?" he asked
me.

"I want to have a talk with your brother," I said.
"But I don't want to ride down into No Name and
get myself shot. So I want you to go in there and get
him. Bring him out to me for a little visit. But I ain't

going to let you go unless you give me your solemn word of honor. What do you say?"

"Well, all right," he said, and I remember wondering if he really meant it or was just jumping at a chance to escape and play me for a fool. There was another possibility, too, that come into my mind. He might actual ride into No Name and get his brother and then come back, but come back with killing on their mind. Killing me. Anyhow, I had him lead the way on over to No Name.

Riding along, I said to him, "What I want you to do is this. I want you to find your brother and tell him that I want to have a talk with him. Tell him I think I've figgered a way out of this thing for all of us. But he's got to come out and see me with just you and him. No one else. You've got to get him to promise you that before you bring him out to where I'm at."

"Okay," Jug said.

Now, if either Jug was lying to me or Snake Eyes should lie to Jug, I was going to be in a pretty bad way when they come out to where I would be waiting. I would just have to be prepared for that possibility. We rode a spell without saying nothing. Then Jug said, "Barjack, what did you mean when you said you had a way of working things out for all of us?"

"You'll know when I see old Snake Eyes," I said.

"Can't you tell me now?" he said.

"I reckon I could," I said, "but I ain't going to. You'll hear it when he hears it." And just then I heard my old guts rumble a mighty protest regarding their hunger. "Another thing I want you to do, Jug, whenever you go in there, I want you to bring us out a steak dinner. Reckon you can do that?"

"Sure," he said. "Barjack?"

"Yeah."

"What makes you think you can trust me?"

"Hell, Jug," I said, "I been asking myself that same damn fool question, and I'm damned if I come up with a answer that makes any sense. For some reason, though, I ain't worried about you. It's your brother what's worrying me."

"Aw, don't worry 'bout old Snake Eyes," Jug said. "If he makes a promise to me, he'll keep it for sure, and if he don't promise me, well, I just won't bring him on out to you, that's all."

Well, I guessed that was some comfort, but I wasn't sure how come. We rode on just a little farther then, and when we sudden topped a little rise, Jug hauled back on his reins. "There she is," he said, and I looked down into a little valley onto the place that they called No Name.

Chapter Twelve

We looked around a bit and found me a fairly comfy spot to relax and wait in, and I sent old Jug off on his own what you call recognization to ride on down into No Name there and find old Snake Eyes and bring his ass on back up to pay a little visit on me. I snuggled myself down against a big rock and got as comfortable as I could get under the trying circumstances, and I lit myself a cigar and uncorked my bottle. I was hungry as all hell, and I sure did hope that the smoke and a drink or two would take my mind off my belly. It didn't work, but the cigar was good and so was the whiskey.

Setting there and waiting like that, I found my mind wandering some. 'Course, I was wondering and worrying a bit about what would happen when old Jug come back with his brother—if he come back. For some reason I believed that he would and that my scheme would work out all right. Now, I knowed well that old Snake Eyes could blast me all to hell if I was to stand up face-to-face with him, but I never figgered on doing nothing that damn foolish.

I had me a good view of the way from where I was at all the way down into No Name, and so whenever they started on their way up to see me, I would get behind the big rock I was a-leaning on and lay my rifle over the top and make damn sure that their intentions was honest and open. That would be just a precaution, 'cause I really and truly trusted old Jug to do right by me. After all, we had had us a few good drunks together by that time.

So I thought I had all that covered pretty good, and I tuck myself a drink, and my mind wandered on back to that bunch of passengers on the stagecoach. I got to tell you that they was bothering me something terrible. I wasn't so sure if it was any of my business at all, but blame it on my job. I was suspicious. It had got into my nature, I guess. But they was something phony about the whole bunch of them. Them two ladies was in a almighty hurry to get on to Denver, even knowing that there was danger ahead, and they both acted so ladylike, they reminded me of my Lillian when I first knowed her. But I figgered that they was something else underneath it, just like there was with Lillian. And then the old lady had showed me there was. But even after that magnificent revelation, there was still something more to be knowed about them, and I wanted to know it.

And then there was the preacher. He was ever' bit

as anxious to face unknown peril as them two women was. And I had found out total by accident that he hadn't even packed hisself no extra clothes for his trip. It seemed to me that he had left Asininity awful sudden-like. But of all of them, the one that was really the biggest puzzle in my damn overworked mind was that little sissy Van Pelt. I'd have thought that he would be the first one to run into a hidey-hole if there was any sign of trouble, but just like them others, he had chose to ride right straight on ahead, right into the gunfire of the whole entire goddamned Snake Eyes gang. It was a major puzzle to me, I can tell you.

Well, I told you, didn't I, that my mind had commenced to wandering, and the next thing it wandered on over to was the question of what was happening back home. I seen images of my horrible kid running wild in the streets and harassing folks, and images of Happy Bonapart a-humping happily on old Bonnie. The toughest thing of all, though, was trying to imagine what old Lillian was up to. I thought that she might be spending all my money. I even had the thought that she might pull all our money out of the bank, sell all our business interests and our house, and run away with all of it, leaving me flat ass broke. I thought that if she done that, I sure as hell hoped she tuck the kid with her.

Well, my brain run through all the thoughts it could run through and had started all over again, and I had smoked up two cigars and brung the whiskey level down somewhat in the bottle. I was hungrier than ever, and I begun to wonder if I had been wrong about old Jug. I was thinking about what I would do to him the next time I seen him, if ever I did, when I seen two men on horseback come riding out of No Name. I set up and watched real careful. They was heading in my direction.

I was just about to move around behind my rock when I got myself another idea, but I knowed that I was going to have to work fast. Them two riders, what I figgered was Jug and Snake Eyes, was still looking real little. You see, it had just popped into my mind that if I was do what I had been thinking I would do, it might just look to old Snake Eyes as if I had laid a trap for him, and that could lead to a shooting war, which was the last thing I wanted to get involved in.

Quick-like, I lit up another cigar. Then I went over to where old Butch's horse, still carrying its nasty load, was standing patient, and I pulled my jackknife out of my pocket and opened it up. I cut off a short length of rope from the cinch off of his saddle. It was tight braided and it was thin. I went back to where I had been setting, and I set myself right back down. Then I scooped out a hole right between my legs, and I stuck one end of that piece of rope down the hole and pushed the dirt back in, leaving just only a couple of inches sticking out visible. I had on my Colts, and my Winchester was leaning on the rock beside me, but I just set there casual, puffing on my cigar.

The two riders was climbing the slope all right, headed directly toward me where I waited. I tuck myself another drink and set the bottle down beside me. They come closer, and then I could recognize old Jug.

In a while I could see that Jug wasn't packing no iron, and that relieved me some. Finally they come up close and stopped. "Barjack," Jug said, "this here is my brother. They call him Snake Eyes."

I just set still, and I said, "Climb down boys, and have a drink."

Snake Eyes was looking right at me, and he never moved his gaze, and, by God, his eyes was even snakier than old Jug's was. Jug clumb down first and walked on over and set down. Snake Eyes swung down then and joined us, but he moved awful slow and cautious. I could tell that he had a suspicious nature. I tuck a drink, so Snake Eyes would know it was okay, and then I handed the bottle to Jug. He sucked on it and offered back to me, but I didn't take it. I nodded at Snake Eyes, and Jug give him the bottle. Snake Eyes tuck a drink, and then I figgered that ever'thing was going to work out all right.

"So you're Barjack," Snake Eyes said. He give me back my bottle.

"I'm Barjack," I admitted.

"You've killed some of my best men," he said.

"They didn't give me no choice," I said, and I never bothered telling him that I hadn't actual killed them all just by my own self. I'd had pretty much help along the way, but I figgered it was all right to let old Snake Eyes think on what a bad ass I could be.

"You the man that wiped out the Bensons?" he asked me.

"Oh," I said, "you heard about that, did you?"

"I heard about it," he said. I tuck another drink and

then give him the bottle. He tuck it and drank. Then Jug reached over and helped hisself to it. "I sent them men after you," Snake Eyes said, "because I heard that you was taking my little brother here back over to Denver to hang."

"Hell," I said, "I know that. And I don't blame you none for it. I wouldn't have no respect for you if you hadn't tried to save your brother's ass from hanging. 'Course, me being a lawman, I couldn't let them take him."

"Well," Snake Eyes said, "I reckon I wouldn't have no respect for you if you had. I got a question for you, though."

I said, "Shoot."

"That's just it," he said. "What's to keep me from shooting you dead right now?"

"You promised me you wouldn't," Jug said, sounding real indignant.

"Hush," Snake Eyes said.

I tuck a puff on my cigar and got its head real bright red, and with my left hand I reached down between my legs. I put a couple of fingers underneath the piece of thin rope and kind of lifted it up to bring attention to it, and with my right hand I lowered my cigar down close to it. "You heard about the Bensons," I said. "Did you hear how I tuck them out?"

Old Snake Eyes's eyes opened real wide when he seen that phony fuse, and I figgered that he had heard all right. I usual tried to make folks think that it was the Bensons what had blowed up Asininity with dynamite, but the truth of what had happened there had got out too, so most people wasn't real for sure just

161

who the hell it was that had done all the blasting.
"You're sitting right on top of that," Snake Eyes said.

I said, "If I go, I mean to have me some company."

"How come you brought me up here?" Snake Eyes
said.

"Did you bring me a goddamned steak?" I said.

"It's cooking," Snake Eyes said. "If we all leave
this hillside alive, we'll go down into No Name and
have ourselves a meal together."

"I wish you'd brung it up here the way I asked you
to do," I said, and I give old Jug a hard look, and he
kind of ducked his head in shame.

"I ain't sure why I brought myself," Snake Eyes
said. "Let's talk."

"You see that horse over there packing that bundle
on its back?" I asked, and I nodded toward the horse
with the putrid remains of old Butch tied onto its
saddle. He nodded.

"That's Butch," Jug said.

"Well," I said, and I pulled out the wrinkle-up
dodger I was still carrying on old Jug out of my
pocket, and I handed it over to Snake Eyes. "You take
a look at what's inside that bundle and tell me, if I
was to take that to the marshal in Denver, could he
tell that it ain't really old Jug here?"

Snake Eyes looked at Jug's picture on the wanted
poster, and then he looked at me. He got up and
walked over to where that miserable horse was standing, and he unloosed the pukey bundle and dragged
it on down to the ground. Then he unwrapped the
blankets just enough till he could see the face there.
He come back over to where I was setting, and he set

back down and looked again at old Jug's picture. Then he looked at me again.

"Are you suggesting," he said, "that you take Butch there into Denver and claim it's Jug?"

"That's my idea," I said.

"Why would you do that?" he said.

"Well," I said, "there's two good reasons. First off, I kind of tuck a liking to old Jug along the road. We come to be pretty good drinking partners. I ain't real anxious no more to turn him over to the hangman."

"All right," Snake Eyes said, but he didn't really sound like he was convinced.

"Second," I said, "I ain't real happy with the thought of getting into a shooting war with you and what you got left of your gang. Now, I got to settle with the marshal in Denver. This here way, I figger all of our problems will be solved, and no one will be hurt by it, and no one will ever be the wiser. What do you say?"

I offered the bottle to Snake Eyes. He set there a-thinking for a space, and then he tuck it and had his-self a drink. He handed it back and stood up. "Let's go have ourselves some steaks," he said.

Well, we all mounted up and rode down into No Name, and old Snake Eyes even insisted that we bring along the extra horse with old Butch throwed back over its saddle. I suggested that it might likely offend some nostrils down there, but that didn't seem to matter none to him. He stopped in front of a little shack, and a feller come out to see what he wanted. I seen deer heads and antlers and some elk heads and even one stuffed bear out in front of the place. Old Snake

Eyes dismounted and went over to talk to the man some, and then they walked together over to Butch's horse, and Snake Eyes lifted up the blanket. The man nodded, and Snake Eyes mounted up again and led us away, leaving Butch and his horse there. Now, Butch was what I was planning on taking into Denver.

"What was that all about?" I said.

"You don't want to take that stinking mess all the way to Denver," Snake Eyes said. "Old Hooter can fix it up real good for you."

We rode on over to another place and had us a real fine steak dinner, and old Snake Eyes even paid for it all. Then we got to drinking whiskey. Hell, pretty soon it was like we'd all been best friends for a good long while. Two or three of Snake Eyes's boys joined us after a while, and old Snake Eyes introduced me like I was his new best friend, 'cause I had saved his brother's life. We all got along real well till Dooley Thompson come in.

Snake Eyes give me the same intro to Dooley as he had to the others, but Dooley never stuck out his hand. He set down and scowled and had hisself a drink or two. Then, of a sudden, he said, "I don't like it, Snake Eyes. This son of a bitch is not only a lawman, he's killed some of our men, including old Butch. I always liked old Butch, and besides that, he owed me some money."

"Forget it," Snake Eyes said.

"It's hard to forget a thing like the killing of a friend," Dooley said.

"Hell," Snake Eyes said, "old Butch was always an asshole, and you know it."

"That ain't no way to talk about the dead and departed," Dooley said. "I say we kill this law dog."

"You ain't the one to say what goes on around here," Snake Eyes told him.

"You ain't the king neither," said Dooley.

Well, as much as I'd had to drink, I could still see that something was boiling, and it was all just over my presence there in their company. Hell, it 'most made me feel real important. Old Dooley was setting right across the table from me, and real slow and sneaky like, I slipped my right-hand Colt out of its holster and aimed it underneath the table at Dooley.

"Barjack here is my guest," Snake Eyes said, "and I ain't going to have you causing him no trouble."

"A low-down piece of dirt like him ain't no trouble, Snake Eyes," I said. "If he wants to start some trouble with me, let him start it."

Dooley went for his gun and started to shove his chair back at the same time, and I pulled the trigger. He screamed something awful, for my shot had tore into his crotch, and both his hands went down there. He leaned over the table, and when he looked up at me with a world of unbelief on his face, I shot again, this time into his chest. I put my Colt away then and waited to see what was going to happen next. Snake Eyes just looked at the two other gang members setting there and told them real calm, "Get him out of here." And they did.

"Sorry to be thinning your ranks like that," I said to Snake Eyes, "but he was for sure wanting to kill me."

"If you hadn't done it, I would have," Snake Eyes

said, and he poured me and him each another drink. "I ain't going to be pulling no more big jobs, though," he said. "Not till I do me some recruiting. Say, Barjack, how would you like to throw away that badge of yours and join up with us?"

Well, that was a hell of a compliment coming from old Snake Eyes, one of the meanest, most wanted, and most feared outlaws in the West. And him trying to get me killed all the way from Asininity to No Name, too. I think I kind of blushed a little bit, and I grinned and ducked my head. "Aw, Snake Eyes," I said, "I couldn't hardly do that. Hell, I got me too good a setup back home in Asininity. I'll tell you what, though. If things ever gets too hot for you around these parts, and you need yourself a nice quiet place to hang out, you and your boys just ride on over to Asininity. I'm the law there. Hell, it's my town. I'll guarantee you a safe stay, as long as you don't pull nothing illegal in my town."

"Why, thanks, Barjack," he said. "That's a right kind offer, and I'll for sure keep it in mind."

"Say," I said, "you got a doc in this place?"

"Old Doc Henry," Snake Eyes said. "Why? You sick?"

"Naw," I said, "but I damn near shot your brother's arm off, before we got to be friends, and it was just patched up by amateurs. I'm thinking he ought to have it looked at by a real doc."

"Aw, hell," Jug said. "I'm all right. It ain't hurting near as much as it did."

"Barjack's right," said Snake Eyes. "Come on. We're going to see Doc."

166

He stood up, and so did Jug. I grabbed the bottle we had been drinking from by its neck and followed them out. As we was crossing the street, I seen the stagecoach coming in. A fat, sweaty, bald-headed man was running to meet it, waving a piece of paper in his hand. "Hey," he said, "is there a Marshal Barjack on board?" I looked over at old Snake Eyes.

"Who's that?" I said.

"He runs a telegraph office here," he said, "Looks to me like you got yourself a wire message."

Snake Eyes kept going toward the doc's office with Jug, but I went to see the fat man. "I'm Barjack," I said.

"Oh," he said, looking around to see if he could figger why I hadn't come off the coach. "Well, this come for you," and he handed me the paper. Well, I read it, and it damn sure answered a big question that had been in my mind for the whole entire trip. I kind of grinned, and I walked over to the stage. The passengers was just piling out, and I stood there till Van Pelt come out ass first. When he had both feet on the ground and turned around to head for the station house, I stood in his way.

"Oh," he said. "Hello, Marshal, I thought that you were gone."

"I was," I said, "for a spell," and I noticed that the little runt was still clutching that bag tight up against his little pigeon chest. "You ain't had no more of them road agents bother you, have you?" I asked him.

"No," he said. "It's been a quiet trip since—"

"Since I left the stage?" I added.

"Well, yes," he said, "but I—"

167

"Never mind that," I said. "Being a duly sworn officer of the law, I was just kind of worried about that there bag you seem to be so concerned about. I was wondering if it was safe enough. You carrying all them important bank papers and all, and going on a real important job for the bank all the way to Denver."

"Uh, thank you, Marshal," he said. "The papers are quite safe."

"You sure?" I said. "Maybe I better have myself a quick look and just be sure."

"No," he said, clutching the bag even harder. "They're all right, I assure you."

Then I stuck that there wire message right up in front of his eyes, and I said, "Let me see, Pelty."

Seeing what was wrote down there, he just kind of sagged, and I pulled the bag loose from his grip and opened it up, and just like I expected, after having read that there message, his little bag was stuffed plumb full of the bank's money what he had stole and slipped away with. That there story he told us all about going to Denver on the bank's business was all just a big fib what he had made up just to cover his chicken little ass. Sure as hell, he never meant to stop in Denver. I figgered he had planned to head off from there for someplace else where no one would ever find him.

Well, I put the handcuffs what used to be on old Jug onto Pelty's skinny little wrists, and I confiscated his bag full of money. Then I found out there wasn't no jailhouse in No Name. 'Course, I should ought to have expected that. After all, the place didn't really even have no name. Then I sudden had a thought that I might have just made myself a real big mistake. It come to me in a flash that I should ought to have kept myself quiet about old Pelty till the stage rolled on safe into Denver. 'Cause all of a sudden I found myself in the big middle of a community full of outlaws with a bag full of stole bank money. It come into my mind that with that much money at stake, old Snake Eyes might just change his mind about what good friends we had become.

Chapter Thirteen

Well, old Snake Eyes, he paused long enough to give me a look that I didn't like too much, but he went on and tuck Jug on over to see the doc. I tuck Pelty into the station house and found the man in charge. They called him Fuzz. I found a rail inside to cuff old Pelty to, and I told Fuzz that he was my prisoner, and that I'd be back for him in a couple or three days. "Feed him enough to keep him alive," I said. "I'll pay up when I come back through and get him." Fuzz said that he'd do that for me. I decided that I had best sleep the night inside, where there'd be less chance of Snake Eyes and his boys trying to pull something on me. And damned if I didn't go right into the deepest sleep I'd had in quite a spell. When I woke up it was already daylight, and breakfast was being put on the table. I seen Fuzz take a plate over to Pelty.

170

I had meant to get up real early and ride out of town before daylight and before the stage left, but when I smelled all that greasy food I just couldn't do it. I set down and filled me up a plate and et till I was full up. Then I tuck up my valise and Van Pelt's bag of bucks and my Winchester, and as late as it was, I decided to just go on ahead and ride the stage in. They was just starting in hitching up the horses, so I figgered I'd have time to find old Snake Eyes. I needed to see him before I left. I had gone outside and was fixing to go hunt him down when I seen him coming. He was carrying a gunnysack in his right hand, and he was a right-handed gun, so I figgered that if he was going to try something, he wouldn't be doing it just yet. I walked over to meet him.

"Going out on the stage, are you?" he said.

"Yeah," I said. "Ain't no need to go horseback this part of the trip. How's old Jug's arm?"

"Doc says it'll mend," Snake Eyes said. He held the sack out toward me, and then he opened it up wide so I could look inside, and there, by God, was Butch's head. "I told you that old boy does good work," he said. "Hell, it don't even stink no more. You can carry it right on the stage with you."

"I'll be damned," I said. "Well, you can tell old Jug for me that this here will make him officially dead and not wanted by the law no more."

"I'll tell him," Snake Eyes said. "We appreciate it." Then he eyeballed old Pelty's bag. "What about that?" he said.

"I'm hanging on to it till I get back home," I said. "Then it'll go back to the bank where it come from."

"You be coming back through here?" he asked me.

"Hell, yes," I said. "I got me a new prisoner in there to pick up and take back with me, and besides all that, I figgered on getting drunk with you and old Jug one more time. Where the hell is old Jug?"

"He was still sleeping when I come out," Snake Eyes said. "I didn't want to wake him up."

Goose Neck hollered, "All aboard," and I excused myself and tuck my stuff on over to the stage. I had done filled up my pocket flask, so I just put my valise with the extra bottles in it back in the boot, but I tuck my Winchester, the money bag, and the sack with old Butch's head inside the coach with me. I couldn't afford to lose them things. We didn't pick up no new passengers there in No Name, so it was just me and Harp and them two Purdy women. The old lady smiled when I got in.

"Glad to have you back with us, Marshal Barjack," she said. The preacher scowled and looked the other way. Young Purdy smiled and nodded.

"What happened to your prisoner, Marshal?" she asked.

"Oh," I said, figgering that was as good a time as any to start building up my story, "some of that there Snake Eyes gang came at me out on the prairie. He wound up dead, so I got his head right here." I hefted the sack. The Purdy women sucked in their breath like as if they was horrified, and Harp turned purple in his face.

"This is absolutely the last straw, Barjack," he said. "This is utterly intolerable."

"Hell, I got to turn him in at Denver, don't I?" I

172

said. "Would you ruther I had shoved his whole entire bloody body in here with us?"

For a while Harp yelled at Goose Neck, trying to get him to stop the stage, but Goose Neck had got used to that. He just ignored him and kept us rolling along. Final the preacher shut up. I thought that maybe he had wore his damn voice out. Then of a sudden I heard a shot from behind us. Goose Neck whipped up the team, and we really started racing down the road. There was another shot, and I heard a voice yell out, "Stop the stage." I stuck my head and right arm and shoulder out the window with my Colt in my hand, and I could see the son of a bitch a-coming up fast behind us. He was close enough to recognize if I'd a knowed him, but I was pretty sure that I had never saw the man before.

I kind of pointed my Colt back towards him and squeezed off a shot, more to let him know that he was facing some opposition than to really try to hit him, for the coach was bouncing something awful. I couldn't have hit the side of a barn. About then his horse stumbled, and he went flying through the air. I figgered that either his horse had broke a leg or else he had broke his fool neck, and that would be the last of him. So I settled my ass back down, and I reloaded that one chamber what I had emptied. Then I got to thinking about the looks of that feller.

I told you that I had never before saw him, but then there was something vague familiar about him. Whenever I first heard the shot, why, a course I thought that it would be one of old Snake Eyes's boys coming after that bank money. So when I looked out the window and seen that it wasn't none of them, I told myself that I had never saw this one before. But I had saw him somewhere—sometime. I just couldn't place it. I couldn't call it up to the front of my damned old brain. Well, like old Goose Neck was so fond of saying, the stagecoach had a schedule to keep, so we never even bothered stopping to see who the man was or if he was hurt or killed or what. We just kept on a-going.

Whenever we had gone on long enough to get the excitement of that last running gunfight settled on down again, old Miz Purdy decided to make some conversation. "This has certainly been an exciting trip," she said, "hasn't it?"

I said, "Stagecoach rides is always chancy, ma'am, but this here one stood to be worse than most, what with that Snake Eyes bunch waiting for us all along the way. That's the reason I tried to get you all to turn around away back yonder."

"That man who just shot at us back there," said the young one, "was he one of that gang?"

"No, ma'am," I said. "I got a good look at him, and I don't believe that he was. Besides, he was a rank amateur. No real professional robber would ever try to chase a stagecoach down from behind."

"Did you shoot him?" said the aunty.

"I think his horse just tripped and throwed him is all," I said, "but he won't be back. It'd be a wonder if one or both of them wasn't hurt. They tuck a bad fall."

"Shouldn't we stop and render assistance?" the preacher said.

"Hell no," I said. "That's what the son of a bitch gets for trying to hold up the stage."

"I should have expected that uncharitable attitude from you," he said.

I guess young Miz Purdy wanted to change the subject or something, 'cause she said, "Wasn't it a shock about Mr. Van Pelt?"

"We must all be on constant guard," Harp said. "The Devil can get his clutches into anyone."

"Well," Idabelle said, "I was certainly surprised. He seemed like such a meek little man."

"The good book says that the meek are going to inherit the earth, don't it?" I said. "I reckon old Pelty just wanted to hurry his share along a bit. Anyhow, I knowed something was wrong with him the way he was a-clutching that there little bag to his chest all the time. And he was in a surefire hurry to get going. 'Course, so was all the rest of you."

"And just what did you mean to imply by that statement?" the preacher said.

"Not a damn thing, Preacher," I said. "It's just only that, like the rest of you tuck note of, old Pelty is a meek little runt, and I got my suspicions up when he wasn't scared of riding into some possible fights with the Snake Eyes gang. I figgered he must be more scared of something back home. That's all."

"But you implied something about the rest of us," Harp said.

"Well, if you really want me to go on about it," I said, "it does seem some peculiar to me that none of you wanted to turn back. It seems to me that ladies and a preacher has to be pretty desperate to face the

kind of stuff we been facing along this road. And you
did get out of Asininity in a hurry, Preacher. You
never even packed no extra britches, did you?"

Well, he purpled up again, and he blustered some,
and then he said, "My packing is none of your business, and I still accuse you of complicity in the theft
of my trousers."

"Now, Preacher," I said, "I ain't admitting nothing
about that, but I would say that if old Jug was in
desperate need of a pair of bitches, you, with your
powerful sense of Christian charity, ought to have
been happy to have furnished him with a pair."

Just then I heard another shot, and then I heard Ash
Face calling my name. "Barjack," he yelled. "Barjack." I stuck my head out the window and stretched
my neck up toward Ash Face.

"What?" I said.

"It's that same feller," he said. "We're going to
have to slow this stage down so we can kill the bastard." I told him to tell Goose Neck to go on ahead
and slow it down. Then I changed my mind.

"Go on and stop it," I said. I picked up my Winchester and cranked a shell into the chamber. The
stage rolled to a rocking stop, and I clumb out in a
hurry. I got down on one knee and tuck myself a bead
on the bastard. It was the same one, all right, riding
the same horse. I reckoned it was a miracle, and I
meant to tell the preacher about it after I had killed
the road agent. I squeezed off a round, but I missed
him.

His hat went flying, though, so I thought that
maybe I had come that close that I knocked it off. I

jacked the lever of my Winchester and went to set up for another shot, but the rider stopped. He just set there on his horse in the middle of the road, looking at me. I had my sites on him, but with him just setting there like that, I didn't really want to shoot him off his horse. I lowered my rifle and stood up. We still just looked at each other. I tuck me a few steps toward him. Still he just set there.

"Hey, you," I yelled. "What the hell do you want? You keep trying to rob this here stagecoach, I'll kill you dead as a dog."

"I ain't trying to rob it," he said. "I just want to stop it."

"Well, by God, it's stopped now," I said. "Hold up your hands and ride on in."

He stuck his hands up over his head, but he was still holding a six-gun in his right hand.

"Empty," I said, and he dropped the six-gun. He rode on up and stopped close to me. Then I realized just who the hell he was. I knowed him, all right. He was a dirt farmer who lived some miles out from Asininity, and he never got into town much. That's how come it tuck me so long to figger out who he was. "Marvin?" I said.

"Yeah," he said.

"What the hell are you up to?" I asked him.

"I never meant to do no robbery," he said. "All I done was just try to stop the stage."

"You was shooting at us," I said.

"I was just shooting in the air," he said. "Trying to get the driver's attention. That's all."

"Well, you sure as hell got all our attention," I said.

"What the hell you want to stop the stage for?"

"I want that Preacher Harp," he said, "for screwing my Nellie."

I guess my jaw dropped down to my chest. Whenever I recovered, I looked back over my shoulder, and I seen Harp trying to sneak out of the coach and over to the side of the road. I don't know where the hell he thought he was going, but he sure didn't want Marvin getting ahold of him. "Well, have at him, by God," I said, and Marvin kicked his horse in the sides and rode hard at Harp. Just before Harp would have got into a clump of trees, old Marvin broadsided him with his horse, knocking him down on his ass.

"Wait. Wait, Brother," Harp called out.

"Don't call me brother, you Bible-thumping son of a bitch," said Marvin, and he was jumping down off his horse at the same time. Harp was trying to get up on his feet, but they was slipping on loose rocks, and he was only half up whenever Marvin pulled off his belt and started whipping him. Harp screamed and hollered. "Barjack," he hollered. "Save me." I laughed out loud, and I said, "I reckon I ought to save you, Preacher, since you saved me back down the road, but this is just too damn much fun."

Marvin kept on a-whipping on him, and the preacher laid down on his face and covered up his head. Old Marvin dropped down astride of him and rolled him over. He commenced to slapping old Harp's face, first one cheek and then the other. Harp put his hands over his face trying to protect it, and then old Marvin, he slid down a ways and grabbed the waistband of the preacher's britches and ripped them open. Then he stood up, grabbed the bottom of each leg, and pulled them britches right off the preacher.

"Stop it. Stop it," the preacher screamed. But old Marvin never stopped a bit. He never stopped till he had the preacher stark staring nekkid.

"Oh, Lord, have mercy," Harp cried out.

Marvin stood up and looked around. He found his belt where he had dropped it there on the ground close by where the nekkid preacher was laying and praying. Of a sudden, old Harp realized that he wasn't being held down and wasn't being beat no more, and he scrambled up to his feet. Just then, Marvin had picked up his belt, and he went to flailing that preacher some more. The preacher run for the woods, and Marvin run after him, a-whipping his ass as he run. The preacher was hollering like a goddamned whooping crane. The two of them disappeared, and I just stood there in the road a-laughing till I hurt real bad on my insides. Goose Neck and Ash Face was laughing, too, but the two ladies was acting kind of like they had just witnessed something awful. I sensed, though, that they would like to have gone ahead and laughed out loud.

Final, we settled down somewhat. "So that's what the preacher was running from," I said.

"I've never witnessed anything so disgraceful," the young Miz Purdy said.

And I said, "Yeah, but it was a hell of a lot of fun, weren't it?" I seen Aunt Idabelle grin a little then, but she never said nothing. "Well, folks," I said, "we have just witnessed justice being done on a grand and glorious scale. And I sure as hell ought to know about justice, 'cause it is my business. That goddamn hypocritical bastard Harp has final and for all time got just what was coming to him. Well, almost."

I went over to where his clothes was laying by the road, there where Marvin had tore them off of him, and I picked them up, ever' last stitch, the britches, the shirt, the coat, the shoes and socks, and the long johns, and I throwed them up on top of the stage. I left his hat laying there. "Let's get going," I said. "We have a schedule to keep." I clumb inside, and Goose Neck, still laughing like hell, whipped up them horses, and we tuck off like blazes on our final leg to Denver.

Well, we rode on for a while without saying nothing more, and then I commenced to laughing again. I just couldn't help myself. I don't think that in all my born days I ever seen anything that I tuck such pleasure in. And I ain't seen nothing since. I got control of myself then, but in just a few miles, I done it again, and this time young Miz Purdy tittered a little, and then Idabelle burst out a-laughing. We all laughed as hard as we could then till we was just about to roll down off the seats into the floor of that coach. We didn't stop till we had to, till our very lives was in danger from all that laughing. When we settled down again final, and it got kind of quiet in there, as quiet as it can get in a stagecoach rolling along a rough road, I sudden heard laughter coming from up on the box.

Well, I tell you, I ain't never seen old Harp again, but now and then I see an image of him appearing from over some distant horizon. He's long and lanky, and he's nekkid as the day he was born. He's walking along slow and sad, and he's got a hat on his head. That's all. I'd sure like to see him again, though. Oh, I wouldn't pick on him or tease him or nothing like that. I'd like to buy him a drink of whiskey and find out if he'd set down with me and drink it. I kind of wonder sometimes if that experience sort of humanized him somewhat.

Well, whatever it done for the preacher, that little episode really loosened up the rest of us, and me and them two ladies had us some good conversation riding along the next several miles. I was feeling good, for by then I knowed why Pelty and Harp had been so anxious to go on ahead, but a course, I still didn't know nothing more about them two ladies. I didn't press it, though. I just carried on casual conversation with them, and now and then we'd all laugh again about the preacher.

One time when we got some quiet, the young one said, "Mr. Barjack, do you really have Mr. Marlin's head in that sack?" I reached down and lifted up the sack off the floor where it had been setting between my feet.

"Yes, ma'am, I surely do," I said. "Would you like to see it?" She turned her head real quick-like and put a hand up over her eyes.

"Oh, no," she said. But Idabelle surprised the hell out of me.

"I would," she said. Well, my bluff was called. What could I do? Besides, it would be the first test. They had rode a good long ways with old Jug.

I opened up that sack, and then I reached in and tuck me a handful of hair, and I pulled that head out. Young Miz Purdy, in spite of her protestations, tuck herself a look. She turned away real quick and made a noise that meant she was some disgusted, but Idabelle stared right at it. Now, because of the time the body had been ignored and the way it had been killed and all that, the face was some disfigured, you know. And I don't know what kind of process it had gone through at that head fixer's shop. Anyhow, after she had stared at it a bit, Idabelle just said, "Yes." I dropped it back in the sack.

It was done dark when we final pulled into the station in Denver. Goose Neck got down and handed out all the baggage. I was standing there with my valise, my Winchester, Pelty's bag of the bank's money, and Butch's head in a sack. And I didn't rightly know where I was a-going. I seen a man come hustling up toward the Purdy ladies.

Chapter Fourteen

Well, I kind of shuffled myself around a bit, making sure that I was close enough to hear what they might have to say to each other, and then that man said, "Welcome, ladies. The stagecoach made it in good time. I have a buggy waiting over here that will get us to the railroad station on time for the train to San Francisco."

"Oh, thank goodness," said the young Miz Purdy. "We had such a trip. I was afraid we'd be delayed."

"And miss your engagement at the Palace?" the man said. "Nothing would dare prevent the appearance there of the great Emma Purdy. Well, let me have those bags. The buggy's right over this way."

Well, as the ladies hustled away with that feller, I watched them go, and I told myself, I'll be damned. Them two hadn't been running from nothing after all.

They was running to something, and that young one was some kind of a star performer on the stage, a singer or an actress, I reckoned. So final I knowed the whole story behind why ever'one on the damn stage was in such an all-fired hurry and how come they was all willing to face just about any kind of danger along the way. My mind was somewhat relieved with all that knowledge. The image of the preacher come back in my mind while I was standing there all by my lonesome, and I couldn't help myself. I chuckled out loud.

It was late, and I seen that there was a hotel across the street and down the way just a little. I was some overwhelmed at all the people and horses in that place. They was buggies and wagons running both ways along the street, men on horseback and men and women afoot hurrying around like they had real important places to get to. I watched real careful and started across the street, but even so I had to dodge a couple of riders and one buggy to keep myself from getting knocked down and rode over.

I made it to the hotel all right and went inside. I signed up for a room for the night, and a young feller in a funny suit tried to take my stuff away from me. I final let him carry my valise, but I hung on to old Pelty's bag and the sack with Butch's head in it. Pretty soon he let me in my room, tuck my valise in there, set it down, handed me the room key, then stood there with a smug look on his face and his hand stuck out at me, palm up. I put the sack and the bag down and just stared right back at him. He didn't say nothing. Final, I said, "What?"

"It's customary to tip, sir," he said.

"You mean you want me to give you some money?" I said.

"It's customary, sir," he said.

"For what?" I said.

"Why, because I carried your bag up here for you, sir," he said.

"Why, you silly little runt," I said, "you practical dragged that bag away from me. I never asked you to tote it. Get on out of here before I tip you on over."

Well, he got out, all right, and I shut the door and locked it. Then I stowed old Butch and Pelty's bag underneath the bed. I opened up my valise to hunt myself another bottle, but I found out that I had done used the last one. I pulled the flask out of my pocket and opened it up, but it didn't hardly have even one good drink left in it. I tipped it up, but all it done was to just make me want some more. I tossed it on the bed and walked out of the room, shutting the door and locking it behind me. Then I went back downstairs.

The little runt in the funny suit was standing by the counter, and the clerk was behind it. I walked over there. "Where's the nearest saloon?" I asked. The little runt just folded his arms over his chest and looked away, like as if he hadn't even heard me. I give the clerk a look.

"Down the street to your right, sir," he said. I left that place and turned right. It wasn't too far down to the saloon. It was called Embrey's, and it was kind of fancy, but I went in there anyhow. Them fancy places don't bother me none.

185

My first inclination was to get myself a bottle and go on back over to the room, but there was just so much action in that place, I decided to hang around for a spell. I went up to the bar and ordered myself a bottle and a tumbler. I paid for the whole bottle and poured myself a drink. I was kind of relaxed, you know, for, by God, I had made it alive all the way to Denver, and I had figured out all the passengers' strange behavior. I did still have that bag full of bank money to worry about, and I figgered that my main worry was going to be old Snake Eyes, and I was going to have to deal with that problem on my way back home.

That is, it come to me, *if* I go home. I figgered there was more money in that little bag than all the money I had tied up in Asininity, counting all my bank accounts and my two businesses and probably a couple of years' worth of my salary for marshaling. If I was to just take that little bag with me and keep on going west or go either north or south but just avoid heading back east where old Snake Eyes would be waiting for me, why, I'd solve myself a whole bunch of problems.

I'd have all the money I would ever need, at least for a good long while. I wouldn't have to face old Snake Eyes and his bunch, and I'd never have to see Lillian or the kid or anyone else at Asininity again. I tell you that sounded like a pretty damn good prospect to me just then. Then I got to thinking about that bag of money as if it was already and for real my own money, and that thought made me worry about it even more. I decided I'd better get back over there to the room to watch over it more careful-like. I drained my tumbler and set it down on the bar. Then I picked up my bottle by its neck and headed on back out the door.

First thing I noticed as I walked back into the hotel lobby was that the little runt in the funny suit wasn't nowhere to be seen. I figgered that he was maybe trying to hustle hisself a tip off of someone else after having stole their bags from them and then carried them up to a room. I headed straight for the steps and clumb up real slow to my room, but just as I was turning the corner to walk on down there, I thought I could see that my door was standing just a bit open. I shifted the bottle over to my left hand and slipped out my right-hand Colt with my right. Then I moved slow and quiet on down the hallway.

I laid myself up against the door and shoved it in with my left arm, and then I seen that silly little runt's ass end. His head was underneath the bed. I thought about waiting till he come out with that money bag and then making my presence known to him, but that ass end was just too good a target. I tuck a long stride into the room and then a long hard swift kick. He yelped and went clean under the bed, and he come out on the other side with old Butch's head in his hands. He looked down and seen what he had ahold of, and he screamed again and throwed that head straight up. It come falling down in the middle of the bed and bounced some.

He sure did want to run, I could tell, but I was blocking the door. "What you going to do now?" I asked him. He stammered some, but he never come

187

out with no real words. I put my Colt away. "Hell," I said, "I ain't going to need this." I tuck a step toward him, and he spun quick and throwed open the window and started to climb out. I dropped my bottle and went after him, grabbing him from behind by his belt, and I jerked his ass back into the room and flung him all the way across onto the floor in the doorway. He tried to scramble up to his feet, but I was on him too damn fast.

He wanted up, so I helped him. I grabbed him by his silly jacket and jerked him up to his feet. Then I spun him around and shoved him back against the wall. He sure was scared. He was trembling, and his teeth was chattering. "That there head scare you?" I asked him. "I collect them, you know, and I ain't got one with exactly your color of hair." Then I slapped his face across one side and the other. "You made me spill a whole bottle of whiskey," I said, which of course wasn't true, but it was damn near full, "and I mean for you to pay for it." I slapped his thighs, and I could tell that he had a pocket full of coins in his right pocket. I tuck hold of it by the top opening and ripped it down, practical baring his right leg, and them coins went all over the floor. I looked down at some of them, and I said, "That ought to do it. What is it, anyhow? Tips?"

He tried to answer me. I'll give him that, but he still couldn't make no words come out. Well, if he hadn't a been such a silly little runt I'd have whipped up on him some more, but I was afraid he was fixing to die on me of only just being scared, or at least piss his pants or something messy like that, so instead I just dragged him out in the hall and pushed him down and around the corner till we was at the top of the stairs. Then I just pitched him headlong and watched him bounce his way down to the main floor. I guess he didn't break nothing important, 'cause he got up real fast and run as hard as he could for the front door. The clerk come out from behind his counter and watched him go. Then he looked up to the top of the stairs and seen me standing there.

"What?" he said. "What was that all about?"

"I caught the little runt in my room," I said, "crawling under the bed after my bags what was tucked in there."

The clerk come over to the bottom of the steps and looked up at me. "Mr. Barjack," he said, "I just don't know what to say. Nothing like this has ever happened in this hotel before."

"Maybe just no one ever caught the little runt before," I said

"Well, I—I'm terribly sorry," he said. "Is there anything I can do?"

"I done run him off for you," I said. "But I did have a brand-new bottle of whiskey when I caught him, and I spilled it in the catching of him. You can get me another one and send it up to my room."

"Right away, Mr. Barjack," he said. "What brand?"

"Bulleit," I said.

He said, "I'll have it up to you right away."

I turned on around and headed back to the room. I put old Butch's head away and checked the money bag. It was all right. I tuck off my hat and coat and boots and laid me down on the bed still wearing my

189

Colts. By and by a woman come to the door. She was carrying a bottle of Bulleit. She stepped into the doorway (it was still standing wide open), and she give the door a polite rap.

"Well," I said, "just come right on in."

She come in and she walked clean over to the bed and put the bottle on the bedside table. She was carrying a tumbler too, just like I like to drink out of, and she had a rag of some kind throwed over one arm. She wasn't no spring chicken, but she wasn't as old nor hefty as old Aunt Idabelle, neither. "Would you like me to pour you a glass?" she said.

"Go right on ahead," I said, and she did. As I was setting up to take advantage of my fresh drink, she went over and picked up the bottle off the floor and set it outside in the hall. Then she come back in and mopped up the whiskey off the floor with that rag she had brought along. She throwed it out in the hall too, and then she come back over to my bedside.

"Anything else I can do for you?" she said.

"Well," I said, "just what all might you have in mind?"

"Mr. Jones told me what happened up here with Wally," she said.

"That the name of that silly little runt in the funny suit?" I asked her.

She giggled and said that it was, and then she said, "He told me to bring you this bottle and to see that you were made very happy. It's all on the hotel."

"In that case, sweet honey," I said, "what's your name?"

"They call me Suzy Q.," she said.

190

"Well, Suzy Q.," I said, setting myself up even more and dropping my legs off the side of the bed. "Why don't you make yourself real comfy while I shut us in tight." I stood up and went to the door to shut and lock it. Then I shoved a bureau over in front of it in case the hotel had any more larcenous-minded employees. I went over to the window and looked out. There wasn't no balcony or nothing there. Hell, I thought, I should have let old Wally climb on out like he had tried to do. He'd a fell and broke his fool neck. I left it open for the cool breeze that was coming through. I figgered we'd need it in a little while. Then I turned the lamp way down low. I tuck off my gun belt and hung it on the headboard of the bed.

By then Suzy Q. was plumb out of her clothes and looking real inviting. I seen right away that she was a for-real blond. I mean blond all over, and though she must have been at least thirty-five years old, she still had a shape that would turn a man on end. Well, I pulled all of my clothes off and jumped in the bed with her, and before the night was over, I had done forgive the hotel for the actions of little Wally, I can tell you that for sure.

Come daylight I sent Miss Suzy Q. on her way with a final pat on her nice round ass, and I got myself dressed and ready to go. It come to me that my valise, not having no more bottles in it, weren't near as full as it had been, so I dumped out all its contents on the bed. Then I pulled out Van Pelt's bag, and I emptied the money all down into the bottom of my valise. Then I packed my clothes back in. I still had some room, so I stuffed old Butch in on top and fastened up my valise. All that stuff would be a hell of a lot easier to pack around that way.

There was some whiskey left in the bottle of Bulleit, and I poured that into my flask and tucked it in my pocket. Then I put my hat on, picked up my valise and my Winchester, and headed on out. Downstairs I slapped the room key on the counter, and the clerk popped right up. "Did you have a satisfactory night, Mr. Barjack?" he asked me.

"I surely did," I told him.

"I can't tell you how embarrassed I am about what happened in your room yesterday evening," he said. "I've reported the incident to the police. I'm sure they'll pick Wally up."

I said, "Well, I don't rightly care if they do or they don't. He ain't never going to forget what happened to him. I'll bet you on that. Say, can you tell me where to find the U.S. Marshal's Office?"

"U.S. marshal?" he said. "But I told you, I've already reported the incident to the local police. They'll handle it nicely, I'm sure."

"Naw, hell," I said. "I ain't going to report nothing. This here is the business I come to town on. I'm a lawman myself, and I got business with the U.S. marshal."

"Oh, I see," he said, showing some relief. "Well, it's a good way from here. You'll want to catch a hansom cab."

He give an address and then walked outside with me and yelled at an old boy in a fancy carriage what drove right over to where we was standing. Then he give the address again to the driver. He opened the door for me to get in, and then he told that driver, "The fare is on the hotel." We rolled on down the street, and the clerk was right. It was a pretty good ride over to that marshal's office. I hadn't no idea just how big that damn Denver was. Why, I'd a been walking all day if I'd set out to find it on foot. I clumb out when the driver stopped in front of the office, and then I barged right in there. I asked for the marshal, and a deputy setting there said he wasn't in. "What's your business?" he said. "Maybe I can help you."

"My business is with the marshal," I said. "I'm Barjack. Marshal of Asininity."

"Oh, yeah," said the deputy. "I remember. But you're supposed to be bringing in a prisoner, aren't you?"

"I told you, my business is with the marshal," I said. I found myself a chair over against the wall, and I set down and put my valise on the floor between my feet. I leaned my Winchester against the wall beside me.

"Well," the deputy said (he was kind of a young one), "maybe I can find him." He got up and put his hat on his head and hurried out the front door. I tuck out a cigar and lit it up, and pretty soon I had that office all full of smoke, and the deputy hadn't got back yet, so I hauled out my flask and had myself a drink. I was just shoving it back in my pocket when they showed up. They walked right over toward me.

"Marshal Boles," the deputy said, "this is Marshal Barjack."

I stood up when Boles put out his hand, and I shuck it. "You're just in from Asininity?" Boles said.

"Late last night," I said.

"You're alone," he said. "We authorized a five-hundred-dollar reward to be paid to a Mr. Happy Bonapart."

"Happy's been paid," I said. "What we want now from you is for the town of Asininity to be repaid by you."

"But where's the prisoner?" Boles said.

I reached down and hauled my valise up and set it on a chair. I opened it up and pulled out the sack what contained old Butch's head, and then I kind of rolled him out on the floor. Old Boles's eyes opened up wide, and the deputy said, "Ugh."

I said, "Old Jug there, his brother is Snake Eyes Marlin. I don't know if you knowed that, but anyhow, old Snake Eyes, he tried to stop me along the way from bringing his brother in. We final had us a hell of a showdown, and old Jug here, well, he didn't survive it."

Boles was making a hell of a face a-looking at that head on his office floor. "But why did you—"

"Cut off his head?" I said. "Well, he was shot up something awful, and after a few miles, he begun to be downright unpleasant, if you get my meaning. It just seemed like the best thing to do, that's all. Anyhow, I brung him in to you, and here's all the paperwork." I hauled papers out of my coat pockets, all the papers I had filled out in order to get Happy his reward money, and I showed them to the marshal. He looked them over. Then he went over to his desk and sat down. He tuck a paper out of his desk and was fixing to write on it, but he looked up again, looking across his desk at that head on the floor, and he said to his deputy, "Jerry, do something with that."

Jerry made like he was going to pick it up, but he hesitated like it was a downright unpleasant chore. I started to just stand there and make him do it, but then it come to me that I might be pushing my luck. So far neither one of them had questioned the identity of the head, so I just sacked it up again real quick and then I handed the sack to Jerry. He tuck it and went out the back way. I don't have no idea what he done with it. Boles finished his writing and handed me a paper.

"This authorizes your reimbursement," he said. "If you take it to the bank right across the street, they'll give you the cash."

I tuck the paper and poked it in my pocket. Then I latched up my valise again, picked up my Winchester, and started to the door. I looked back over my shoulder and said, "Pleasure doing business with you, Marshal Boles. Say, ain't you Bill Boles? The one they call Wild Bill?"

"I am," he said, "but just now I don't feel so wild."

I walked on out and walked across to the bank and got my cash. I tucked it in my pocket with the paper that Boles had give me. My business was all done, all except taking the bank's money and Van Pelt back to Asininity. I stood out on the sidewalk for a minute or two, thinking about it. If I was to do them two things, I knowed that I'd cross paths with old Snake Eyes again. I still hadn't made up my mind if I wanted to take that chance. I sure had me a bundle

Robert J. Conley

of money to get lost on if I was of a mind to. I had done broke loose from Asininity and Lillian and all the rest of it. I could stay broke loose for good if I was to really take such a notion.

Chapter Fifteen

Well, I caught me another one of them hansom things and got me a ride back to where I had started off from. I knowed that I would need me some more whiskey than just only what I had left there in my little old pocket flask, so I stopped off at that fancy saloon again and bought myself four bottles. With old Butch done delivered under the name of Jug Marlin there was room in my old valise again. I had me a drink in the saloon to start the day off right, and I stashed them four bottles down inside my valise. It was of a sudden a very precious piece of cargo what with all that good whiskey and all that stole bank money inside. I was trying to decide what to do with myself, so I ordered me up another drink to think on.

I knowed there was a whole wide world out there, and I could go anywhere I wanted on all that money.

I thought about San Francisco, New Orleans, St. Louis, Mexico City, hell, Paris even. I even thought about my own growing-up city, New York, and I knowed that I could go back there with all that money and stay in a better part of town than that part where I growed up and likely never run into none of them goddamn Five Pointers. But if I was to do any of that, I knowed that I'd be striking out on my own all alone, and I'm a man what craves company. I was already feeling the need of someone to get drunk with.

So I commenced to scheming in the other direction. There would be a stagecoach east in just another hour or so, and I could get on it and head back to Asininity. Along the way I would almost for sure run into old Snake Eyes and his bunch. I had thought to stop off and get drunk with Snake Eyes and Jug and them, but that was before I come up with all that bank money, and I figgered that Snake Eyes would go for that money no matter if I had conjured up a way to save his brother's ass from hanging.

When that crucial time come, I would be faced with two choices. Old Snake Eyes would likely tell me that if I was to just hand him all that money, I could move on down the road unharmed. On the other hand, if I was to refuse to do him that one little thing, he'd most likely up and kill me dead, or at least try, in order to get his hands on it. 'Course, he had already invited me to join up with them. That was another option I had, but I figgered that sooner or later Snake Eyes and Jug and all them around them was either going to get caught and dangled from the ends of ropes or else get shot dead trying to avoid being put under arrest. Outlawry had its rewards, that was certain, but its damn near inevitable end wasn't one of them. I shoved that option off to one side immediate. I was a lawman. I wasn't cut out to be no outlaw.

But then it come to me that if I was to run off with that money, that's just exactly what I'd be making myself into. I'd be a fugitive on the run for the rest of my life. Now, if I run off to Mexico City or Paris or someplace else like that, likely I'd be safe enough, but what if I didn't like the goddamn place? What if I was to get a craving to come back to this here country? I wouldn't be able to come back, or else I'd be coming back at risk of life or freedom or something. Well, I figgered that I'd best head back toward Asininity. So the thing was, I had to figger how to get around or through old Snake Eyes.

So I thought real hard, and I thought about how I'd bluffed old Snake Eyes out with just only a short piece of rope cut from a cinch, and then I reminisced about the way in which I had wiped out the whole entire Benson gang almost single-handed. And there I figgered was my answer. Dynamite. Just one stick could take out a whole mess of men, if they was setting close enough together. I downed what was left of the whiskey in my glass and left the saloon.

Just all that thinking had done et up some of the hour I'd had, so I was in kind of a hurry, but I found a place soon enough, and bought me a couple of them powerful blowsticks and tucked them in the inside coat of my jacket. Then I hurried on over to the station in time to board the stage. I started to hang on to my valise, but then I recalled that it was the way old Pelty had clutched his little bag to his chest that had made me suspicious of him in the first place, so I just went on ahead and stashed it in the boot like I had before, like I didn't give much of a damn about it anyway.

I was glad to see that Goose Neck and Ash Face had drawed the return run, and whenever Goose Neck called out for all of us to board the coach, I handed my Winchester up to Ash Face. "I don't reckon I'll be needing this on this here trip," I said. He tuck it and put it in the front boot down under the driver's box, and I clumb on in. Well, the damn coach was plumb full with three of us on each bench facing each other. There was a horse-faced old gal of about forty setting right beside me smelling of scented powder, and on the other side of her was a skinny galoot in a dark suit and high hat what I tuck for a professional gambler. Across from me set a young feller. He could a been a farmer's kid. It was hard to tell. He wasn't yet old enough to have give hisself much of a personal identity yet. Next to him set a fat, sweaty feller in a suit. I tuck him for some kind of a drummer, and I wondered what his wares was. Final there was a young woman, but she was kind of plain and mousy-looking. I figgered it was going to be a drearisome ride, so I was glad I had filled up my flask, and I figgered on getting myself some sleep along the way.

I hauled my flask out and tuck myself a snort, and I noticed out of the side of my head that old lady look down her horse nose at me. I give out a loud sigh of pleasure just to get her goat, put my flask away, and settled myself back for a snooze. It tuck a spell 'cause of the bouncing, but I soon made it all right and drifted off. And I had me a real swirl of dreams what all just run together in my mind after I woke up, but I remember that Lillian and Bonnie was both in there somewhere, along with Jug and Snake Eyes and the bank's money. Anyhow, eventual there come a hell of a bump, and it jolted me all the way back into the real world.

I stuck my head out the window and hollered up to Goose Neck. "Hey," I said, "where the hell are we at?"

" 'Bout three miles out of No Name," he yelled back at me. I thought about having Ash Face pass my rifle back down to me, but then I remembered them blowsticks in my pocket. I figgered that my best defense in front of old Snake Eyes would be to just seem as relaxed as I could. If that didn't work, why, them blowsticks would. I kept looking out the window, and when I final seen No Name just up ahead, I tuck out a cigar and lit it up. The old gal next to me wrinkled her horse nose in disapproval, and I give her a face full of cigar smoke for good measure.

Well, whenever we come to a stop there in front of the station, I clumb down out of the coach, and I didn't even bother fetching my valise out of the boot. I just stood there and stretched for a bit, and then I seen old Jug coming at me with a wide grin on his goddamned face. "Hey, Barjack," he called out. I walked on toward him and met him halfway, and we shuck hands. "I wasn't sure you'd be coming back," he said.

"Hell," I said, "I told you I'd be back, didn't I?

Say, do you realize that you're legal dead? You're wrote down dead in the office of the United States marshal. There ain't no more dodgers out on you, old partner. You're dead. Just think about that."

"Well, I'll be damned," he said.

"You're a clean and free man," I said.

"Barjack," he said, "that's just plain damn wonderful."

"So what's your new name?" I asked him.

"Huh?" he said.

"You can't go around calling yourself Jug Marlin no more," I said, " 'cause Jug Marlin is wrote down dead. You got to have a new name."

"Oh," he said, scratching his head, "I hadn't thought about that."

"Well, think on it," I told him. "Come up with a new name. Hell, it can be anything you want it to be."

"Anything?" he said.

"Sure," I said. "You can be George Washington or Abraham Lincoln. Whatever. Julius Caesar."

"I don't like none of them names," Jug said. "I know. I got it. From now on, I ain't going to be Jug Marlin no more. From now on I'm Jug Martin."

"Jug Martin?" I said.

"Yeah," he said. "You like it?"

"Jug," I said, "I never knowed that you was so clever. By God, Jug Martin it is. Say, where's your— Uh-oh. I like to slipped up there and said your brother. Say, where's old Snake Eyes Marlin?"

"Oh," Jug said, "he's over at the bar a-waiting for me to fetch you in. He's wanting to buy you a drink."

"Yeah?" I said, puffing on my cigar. "I bet he is. Well, what the hell're we waiting for?"

We walked on across the way to the hovel what served No Name for a saloon and went inside. Sure enough, old Snake Eyes was setting there at a table. A bottle of Bulleit was setting there, and there was three glasses. Me and Jug went on over and set down. "Howdy, Snake Eyes," I said.

"How'd you make out?" he asked me.

"Slicker'n hell," I said. "Whenever I rolled that there head out on the floor, that marshal couldn't hardly stand to look at it, much less question its identity. Your brother has been wrote down dead."

"Good," Snake Eyes said.

"I done changed my name, too," said Jug. "I changed it to Jug Martin."

"Hell," said Snake Eyes, "you going to go straight too? Going to go to work in a store? Leave your old brother?"

"What?" Jug said.

"Aw, never mind," Snake Eyes said. He looked at me. "I owe you a thank-you for keeping my brother from hanging." He poured me a tumbler full of whiskey, and I seen that it was that good Bulleit what I especial liked. I waited real polite-like till he poured one for hisself and one for Jug. Then I picked up mine and tuck a long drink from it. "Barjack," Snake Eyes said, "what about the little man in the station?"

"What about him?" I said.

"He for real rob your bank?" he said.

"That's what they say," I said. "He'll get a trial before he's called guilty."

"He have the bank money with him whenever you arrested him?" Snake Eyes asked me.

"He had some money," I said. "It ain't yet been proved to be the stole bank money. That'll be tuck up by the court too."

"How much?" Snake Eyes asked.

I shrugged. "I ain't counted it," I said.

"You got it?" he asked.

"I tuck it away from him," I said. "Tuck it into Denver with me."

"That ain't what I asked you, Barjack," he said.

"That's all I aim to answer," I said. "That there money ain't none of your business. It's my business, the court's business, and the bank's business. I'll tell you this much. I sure ain't got it on me. I left that little bag in Denver."

"With the U.S. marshal?" he said.

"Could be," I said.

"Banks can wire money back and forth or give each other letters or such nowadays, can't they?" he said, but he wasn't really talking to me nor no one else, I didn't think. He was kind of thinking out loud, I guess. Then he said right out, "I don't believe you left that money in Denver, Barjack."

I said, "What do you think, Snake Eyes? You think I stashed it somewheres, and I'm planning on running off to Paris or some damn place like that? Maybe some island with girls what don't wear nothing but grass skirts and swish their butts and jiggle their tits for you? Is that what you think?"

Old Snake Eyes sudden got a faraway look in his watery blue eyes, and he said, "That ain't such a bad thought. Laying around on a beach somewhere. No posses chasing after you."

"I don't know if they got saloons in them places," I said.

"Well, then," he said, "where would you go?"

"I think I'll stay where I know what's what," I said. "I'm on my way back to Asininity. I got me a couple of women there. Got a home and two businesses, and I'm the goddamn town marshal. I don't reckon I could want no more than that."

I tuck me another drink, and that emptied my tumbler, so old Snake Eyes poured it full again. I didn't really like the way the conversation was going, so I tried to change the subject. "How's the arm, Martin?" I said. I didn't get no answer. "Jug Martin?" I said, and old Jug looked up like he'd been asleep and someone had just woke him up real sudden.

"Oh," he said. "I forgot for a minute there."

"Hell, boy," I said, "if you're going to take you on a new name, you got to remember it. Hell, you don't want to be letting the cat out of the bag, do you?"

"I'm sorry, Barjack," he said. "I'll remember from now on."

"Well, you'd best, by God," I said. "If anyone finds out that you're Jug Marlin 'stead of Jug Martin, you'll be a wanted man again and subject to arrest and hanging by the neck, and I'll be in deep trouble, too, for turning the wrong head over to the U.S. marshal. That ain't no small thing, you know, so you and me is in this thing together all the way—Martin."

He hung his head and got a pout on his face and said, "I said I'm sorry."

205

"All right," I said. "How's your arm?"

"It's coming along all right," he said. "Doc told me it's going to mend 'most good as new."

"I'm glad to hear it," I said.

"You know," Snake Eyes said, "we wouldn't have to go to no island. With that much money, we could just go to San Francisco or some big city like that. Hell, no one would know any of us there. We could all change our names and get ourselves city clothes and haircuts and settle down to the good life."

"We ain't going nowhere on that money, Snake Eyes," I said. "That there money is on its way right now back to the bank."

"It is?" he said. "How's it going?"

"I ain't telling you that," I said. "Let's just quit talking about that money. Now, you and me made a bargain. I figgered out how to save your brother, and I done it, and by the doing of it, we made peace between us, you and me. We got drunk together. I figger that makes us friends. I done promised you you'd be safe in my town if you ever come that way."

Snake Eyes tuck hisself a drink and smacked his lips, and then he looked at me with them beady damned eyes. "Barjack," he said, "we made our bargain, and we kept it. We become friends. It's done. Then you come up with all that money, and that's a whole new deal. What kind of a man would hold out on his friends when he come onto a whole bunch of money like that? Huh? You tell me that. What kind of a friend would that be?"

"Goddamn it," I said, "I got my job to do. I'm a lawman. Just being friends don't change that none."

"Well," he said, "I got my line of work too. I'm a stealer of money, and just being friends don't change that none, either."

I turned down my glass and drunk up all the whiskey in it, and I stood up. "This conversation has become unfriendly," I said. "I'm going on back over to the station and get me some shut-eye. I'll be leaving out on the stage early in the morning. See you boys around sometime."

I walked on out of that there bar and walked on back over to the station 'bout half expecting old Snake Eyes to shoot me in the back 'most anytime. I really didn't think he would, though. First off, he didn't know where the money was at. He didn't know if I had left it in Denver or sent it back to Asininity by some sneaky method or if I was carrying it or if I had hid it somewheres. Then there was what I had did for his brother, but that wasn't near as important as the other reason. Anyhow, I must have been right, 'cause he never shot me.

I got back to the station, and I retrieved my Winchester from Ash Face. Of a sudden, I thought I might need it. I thought about my valise out there in the stage boot, and I had myself a little argument in my head. I said to myself I'd be a damn fool to leave it out there unguarded with all that money in it. On the other side, I said, if I was to go get it and hang on to it or set on it, then it would be obvious that I was worried about the son of a bitch, and Snake Eyes or someone would figger it all out. Final I just left it there and went inside the station. This time, I figgered, I'd sleep on the floor with the others.

Robert J. Conley

I laid out a blanket and drunk up most of what was in my flask. Then I stretched myself out and tried to go to sleep, but it wasn't hardly no use. I just laid there a-thinking about old Snake Eyes and wondering what he was scheming up inside his ugly head. I knowed he wasn't going to let a chance at that much money just go by without putting out some kind of effort.

I had him puzzled as to the whereabouts of the money, but he sure as hell knowed where to get his hands on me. I figgered he wouldn't do nothing right there in No Name in front of so many witnesses, but then, I also figgered he wasn't about to let me just ride on out of there unmolested. I wondered if he'd lay an ambush for the stagecoach somewhere along the line the next day. If he was do that, him and all his assholes would be wearing masks. They could haul down on old Goose Neck and Ash Face and make them stop the stage, and then they could grab me off it and take me off somewhere to work me over and make me tell them where the money was at. Leastways, that could be what he was a-thinking. But that kind of thing was the reason I had stashed them two blowsticks in my pocket, too. I just needed to make sure that I had me a cigar going whenever that time come about.

I still couldn't sleep, and my flask was empty, so I got up and walked outside in just my long johns. I went over to the stage, and out of the side of my face I seen old Jug a-hiding in the shadows. I just ignored him. I went right to the stage boot and opened it up. I got my valise and unlatched it and reached in and tuck out a bottle. Then I closed everything up and walked back to the front door of the station carrying nothing but just only that bottle by the neck. I made sure, though, that I seen Jug's reaction. I seen him run off as I was going in the door.

I smiled there in the dark inside of the station house as I was making my way back over to my own particular place on the floor. Jug would go back to Snake Eyes and tell him that I had gone to my valise in the boot and pulled out a bottle. He would also tell him that I hadn't tuck nothing else out of there. Snake Eyes would never think that the money was in there and I had left it unwatched. I figgered the money was safe all right. I tuck myself another drink, and I went to sleep pretty soon after that.

Chapter Sixteen

Well, I can tell you, though, I didn't sleep too good that night. When I was sleeping, I was dreaming about Lillian and the kid. Lillian was griping at me, and the kid was howling around and harassing the hell out of me. When I woke up, I was rassling with ideas. I wondered if I should get back on the stagecoach in the morning. Old Snake Eyes had stopped the coach before. What the hell would keep him from stopping it again? He still had a fair number of hands. 'Course, he didn't know where the hell the money was at. I tried to figger what he would do. I put myself in his place.

If it was me trying to figger out where that money was, what would I do? I asked myself. Would I stop the stage and search it? Would I catch the man what had it, which of course was me, and try to beat the information out of him? I wondered if old Snake Eyes would do that and if Jug would try to stop him. I also wondered how the hell I would hold up to that kind of mistreatment. The thing was, I had to make sure that they never would get me in that kind of situation.

So the question become how to make sure about that. How to keep myself from being caught by them bastards. I was asking myself whether my chances would be better on the stage or on horseback. If I was to be on the stage, Snake Eyes would know just exactly where to find me. That was one thing. But then I'd have old Ash Face to help me stand them off, too. There was that.

On the other hand, if I was to steal myself a horse and just ride on out, they'd have to come looking for me, and they wouldn't know which direction to look in. It would sure as hell take them longer to find me, and maybe they wouldn't never find me at all. Well, hell, I drifted off to sleep again, and had me some more uncomfortable dreams, and then I woke up again, and went right back to them same old thoughts. The idea of Ash Face and his shotgun siding me was sure comfortable, but then, I did have them two blow sticks, and the thought of being out horseback and Snake Eyes and them not knowing where to look for me was comforting too, in a different sort of way.

But all of a sudden I remembered old Pelty over there all cuffed up. Goddamn it. If I was to take out horseback, I'd have to steal myself two horses in order to take old Pelty along with me. And I figgered that I pretty much had to take him along. If I was to take the bank's money back, I had ought to take the bank robber along with it. Then for one last time the thought flashed through my mind that I could just leave Pelty where he was at and ride off on my own in just anywhich direction with all that money and start myself a whole new life somewheres.

On the other hand, I already had myself a pretty good reputation as a tough lawman. I had cleaned up Asininity and wiped out the Benson gang. I would really look like a big shot whenever I rode back into Asininity with a bank robber and all the bank's money. And I had my job and my business interests and Bonnie and ever'thing back there, too. I got up and pulled my boots on. Then, carrying along my Winchester, I slipped real quiet out of the station.

I guess Snake Eyes and them had all drunk their-selves to sleep, 'cause No Name seemed deader'n a goddamned well-did steak. I didn't even see no horses at the hitch rails. Down at the far end of the street there was a stable, though, and I snuck in there. I seen plenty of dead outlaws' horses, and I saddled up a couple of the best-looking ones. I slipped out the back way with them and swung wide around the set-tlement till I got to the back side of the station. I left the horses there.

Next I walked around front and fetched my valise out of the stage boot. I slipped real sneaky-like back inside and over to where I had cuffed Pelty. I found him tossing around trying to sleep. I had put him in a real uncomfortable position, and I clapped a hand over his mouth. His eyes popped open real wide, and I said in a whisper, "Keep quiet, you little bastard or I'll thrash you good." I unlocked the cuff that was holding him there, and I made him slip outside out the back way with me.

I shoved Van Pelt up onto one of the horses, and then I tied his hands to the saddle horn. I tied my valise onto the other saddle and mounted up. Then I tuck the reins to Pelty's mount and led it off. I moved us on out of No Name slow and easy, watching behind me all the time, but pretty soon we was on out of there. I kept us on the road, 'cause it was dark as the inside of a bear's ass. I figgered it wouldn't be too safe getting out in the middle of the damn prairie.

"Barjack," Pelty said, "what are you up to?"

"You'll find out," I told him.

"Are you taking me back to Asininity?" he asked.

"You'll know when we get there," I said.

We rode on a little farther before he spoke up again. Then he said, "Barjack, there's enough money for both of us to live like kings for the rest of our lives. I'll divide it with you."

"Pelty," I said, "you silly little Jackass, if I was to want to steal that money, why the hell would I want to split it with you? You ain't in no position to make no deals. I've got the money, and I've got you. I don't need to divide nothing with you. I don't need to make no deals with you. You just keep your damn mouth shut, and we'll do fine."

Well, I ain't got no idea what time I got up and went to steal them horses, but we rode the rest of that night, and it didn't seem like it was all that long. The skyline along the eastern horizon begun to light up just a bit, and I figgered that old Goose Neck was likely hitching up the team. I figgered, too, that old

Snake Eyes would be up and watching to see me off, and pretty soon he'd realize that I was done gone. Then he'd be after me all right. Him and several others. I kept us on the road a little longer, till it was light enough to see the ground better.

Then I recalled that I had rode off to the north once before, and I figgered old Snake Eyes would recall that too, so I rode off to the south. The landscape down thataway was more uneven with rolling hills, and there was more cover, too, in the form of brush and clumps of scrubby trees. When we couldn't see the road no longer, I figgered we was far enough away, and I turned us back east again, riding as best I could parallel to the road. About then my stomach commenced to grumbling and growling.

I knowed that the stagecoach and then old Snake Eyes and them was at least three or four hours behind us, so I decided that we could afford the time to stop and have a quick meal. I staked out the horses and old Van Pelt and tuck my rifle with me up onto the top of a rise. I seen a whole prairie dog village off down there, and I tuck careful aim and blowed the head off one of them. The others all disappeared right quick. I walked over there and picked up the one I had got, and then I walked back to where I had staked the horses and my prisoner. I picked up sticks along the way, and when I got back there I built a little fire. I let it get good and hot while I cleaned that dog, and then I roasted that dog meat up real good. I cut it up and give some to Van Pelt, but I was careful not to give him none of the best pieces.

I got myself fairly well satisfied on that meal, but

old Pelty picked at his some. "What's the matter with you?" I asked him. "Ain't you hungry?" He looked at me with his nose kind of wrinkled up, and he said, "I've never eaten prairie dog before. It's tough, and it's stringy."

I said, "Out on the trail like this, you need something tough in you to keep you going. You'd best enjoy that. Our next meal is like to be rattlesnake." Well, he like to have gagged on that thought, but he did manage to eat some more of that tough and stringy meat. I put the fire out soon as the meat was cooked, 'cause I didn't want no one spotting us by it. I sure was craving a cup of coffee, but we washed down our dog with water. I got us mounted up and started on our way again. For the first couple of miles, Pelty was making such noises as I thought he would puke, but he never. He held it down.

We was making pretty good time, and so when we come to a rise, the highest one I had yet seen, I held us up there for a minute. I looked back west, and I seen a dust cloud a way on back. I could tell that it was on the road, and I knowed that it was the stage-coach a-rumbling along. I couldn't see nothing else, no smaller dust cloud trailing it or nothing like that, so I didn't have no way of knowing whether or not Snake Eyes was on the trail. I pulled out my flask and tuck a drink. "Goddamn," I said as I put the flask away again. "Let's get going."

"Barjack, wait," Van Pelt said. "Wait a minute. Let's talk about this some more."

"Pelty," I said, "we ain't got nothing to talk about. Get that in your stupid head. Or if you can't get that in your head, then get this: If you don't keep your goddamn mouth shut, I'll stuff it full of a rag to keep you quiet." I kicked my horse into a run and pulled Pelty's along behind. I didn't mean to run them horses long like that, but I just wanted to jerk old Pelty off and give him a scare. In a little bit, I slowed them down to a walk again.

As we rode along, ever' now and then I looked back to see if that dust trail was still a-coming on down the road, and it was, up till about noon, I reckon. The sun was high overhead, and I looked back, and I didn't see no dust rising. I knowed that could mean any number of things, like a busted wheel or a lame horse or a sick passenger, even a road agent, but the way I was thinking, what I thought was, I figgered old Snake Eyes had stopped the stage a-looking for me or the money or both. I hoped that he wasn't going to kill ever'one on it just out of frustration, 'cause, a course, I knowed he wasn't going to find what it was he was a-looking for.

I also figgered that whenever he had searched that entire stage and all the people on it real thorough-like, he'd be hot on my trail, having figgered out that I was horseback and likely guessing that I had the money with me. I wondered if he would notice that my valise was no longer in the boot and realize that he had passed up a chance last night of just picking up all that money and walking away with it. I kind of hoped that he would figger that one out and kick his own ass for about a half a mile.

We rode on some then, and old Pelty must have believed me whenever I threatened to stuff his mouth full of rag, 'cause he kept his yap shut all right. That little bastard was the single chickenest character that I ever had or ever thought to of had for a prisoner to be taking to my jailhouse. Why, hell, if I had yelled real hard at him, I believe he'd have fell over and cried. The more I thought about him, the more amazed I was that he'd ever had the guts to rob the damn bank, even the way he done it, which was to just sneak the money out was all. But folks is always full of surprises, ain't they?

Hell, I was half a mind to give the little bastard a hundred dollars and let him run, but then I figgered turning loose two criminals on one trip would be just too damn much. We rode the rest of that day and into the night, and I made us a little camp, but only without no fire. I didn't have no idea how close old Snake Eyes and them might be by that time, and I didn't want to take no chances. We went to bed cold and hungry, and I was thinking about the meals what was available in them stage stations, but I talked myself out of going back to the road. I figgered the way we was going, it would take old Snake Eyes about a hundred years to find us. I wanted to keep it that way.

The next morning I got bold and made a little fire. I boiled up some coffee and killed a rabbit and another prairie dog, and old Pelty, he stuck to the rabbit. I thought that dog was pretty damn tasty myself, but ever'one has different tastes. We et and drank us some coffee. I put the fire out right away when I was done with it. "Pelty," I said, "how come you to do it? A harmless little feller like you with a respectable job and ever'thing. How come you to steal all that there bank money?"

He kind of shrugged, and then he said, "I don't know, really. I must have been crazy. I think that I just got tired of handling so much money and being paid so little. It just didn't seem right. Why, if I'd only had a dollar out of every hundred I handled, I'd have been rich. I let it eat at my thoughts like that until I just couldn't stand it any longer, and then I planned it, and then I did it. That's all."

"What was you going to do?" I asked him, "if you had got away?"

"I was headed first for San Francisco," he said. "I hadn't really thought much beyond that. I thought that I'd be able to do anything, go anywhere with all that money. It all seemed very beautiful—while it lasted."

"Well, Pelty," I said, "I'm kind of sorry it didn't work out for you. Well, mount up. Let's get going."

Then, as Pelty stood up seeming to do like I told him, I done a real stupid thing, but you see, I thought the little feller was total harmless. I reached over to pick up the can I had used to boil our coffee in, and then I felt a hell of a thud on the back of my head, and I seen nothing but black and a little kind of like stars dancing around in it. I don't think I was clean out, but I was plumb useless. I believe that I heard the sound of the horses' hooves as they was taking off, and I recall asking myself what the hell he could have hit me with. But I was so damn groggy, I was worse than full drunk. I couldn't get up, and I couldn't see. I was just kind of floating around helpless. Final, I just laid down my head and relaxed.

I don't know how long it was, but after a while I come to again. I set up real slow. My head was still hurting and swimming around some. Final I felt kind of steady and I looked around. Sure enough, the little bastard was gone, and so was both horses, my Winchester, and my valise with all the money and my extra whiskey bottles in it. I had been out long enough for him to get clean away. I didn't see no sign of him nowhere. I felt of my pockets, and I still had my two blowsticks and my pocket flask. I even still had my two six-guns in their holsters. I guess the little bastard, once he had knocked me over, was too scared to get too close to me even then, and he had just run for the horses.

Anyhow, there I was. I had two Colts, a little whiskey, no rifle, no water, no food, and no horse. I was somewhere out in the middle of the vast prairie, some few miles south of the nearest road. I sudden figgered that my chances of survival was slim. It's damn hard to hit a prairie dog or a rabbit or any other kind of game with a six-gun. I had no idea where to look for water nor whether they was any settlers around anywhere nearby. I could walk north and eventual hit that road, and then try to figger which direction to go to the nearest station. I'd get food and water there, but then maybe old Snake Eyes would come riding along about then too.

I pulled out my flask and tuck myself a drink, and it did make me feel some better. I set there for a spell to allow that good whiskey to do its work, and it cleared my head some. Then I tuck me another for good measure. Final, I stood up and started walking.

I seen the tracks of the two horses, and they was moving east. Now, I knowed that old Pelty didn't want to go back to Asininity nor any place near it, so I figgered that he was just getting away from the Snake Eyes gang, knowing that they was on my trail. Somewhere along the line, he'd have to turn north or south. But as long as he was still headed east, so did I.

I never was one for walking no farther than I absolute had to, and it wasn't long before I was staggering. I had got blisters on both my feet, and my legs was aching from all that unused-to activity. I was also puffing for air. I tuck off my coat and was trailing it along beside me. Once I thought about dropping it and leaving it behind, but I recalled them two dynamite sticks in the pocket, so I kept ahold on it and kept a-dragging it. I reckon I was leaving a hell of a trail if anyone was to come along to follow it.

When I'd had about all I could take, I laid down to get me some rest, and whenever I woke up next it was near dark. I wondered where Pelty had gone to. I wondered where the stagecoach was and where Snake Eyes was at. I just barely figgered out which direction was north, and I got myself up, a-hurting all over, and I started walking toward the goddamn road. Well, I won't belabor this no more, but I will tell you that I thought I was dead about seventeen times before I found the swing station what saved my life.

I staggered into that place and begged for food and water, and I never told them a goddamned thing till I had et all I could hold, drank about a gallon of water and a couple of pots of coffee, and topped it all off with a good long drink from out of my flask. Well, then I set back and pulled off my boots and propped my tired and sore feet up. I lit myself a cigar and tuck a few good puffs. Then I asked them if old Pelty had come through. At first they didn't even know who I was talking about. I told him he was the silly little banker what had clutched that little bag to his chest all the time on our way out to Denver. Then he come back into their minds.

"Ain't seen him," said one of the station crew. "What you want him for?"

"First off," I said, "that little bag of his was chock full of bank money what he had stole. Second, I had recovered the loot and arrested him and was taking them both back when the little bastard conked me on the back of the head and got away. I had to walk myself damn near to death, 'cause he got the horses too. I'm a-hunting him now."

"Well," the feller said, "if he robbed the bank back where you come from, he wouldn't be heading back that way, would he?"

"I've done thought that one through," I said. "The Snake Eyes gang from up to No Name found out about all that money. They was behind us. I reckon he figgers he's got to get clear of them before he changes his direction again. Say, you ain't had no visits from them outlaws here, have you?"

"No," the feller said. "Ain't had no visitors of no kind."

"Has the stage come through here yet?" I asked him.

"It ain't," he said. "It's due anytime now."

Well, sure enough it pulled in shortly after that, and a course, this here being a swing station, all they was going to do was to just change the horses and let ever'one make a run to the john out back, and then hit the road again. I never even stood up. Goose Neck come in and seen me. He tuck hisself a cup of coffee, and he said, "Barjack, what the hell are you doing here?" Well, I told him the whole damn embarrassing tale, and then I said, "I'm riding back with you now." I asked him if he had seen old Snake Eyes, and sure enough he had.

"He stopped us back yonder a ways," he said. "Made us all climb down off the box or out of the coach, and then him and his boys throwed everything out and went through it all. 'Damn,' he said, 'it ain't here. I ought to kill ever' damn one of you, but that wouldn't do me no good.' Them was his words. Then him and his boys all mounted up again and rode off."

"Which way'd they go?" I asked him.

"Went north," said Goose Neck. "Off the road."

Old Ash Face had come in just a little before that and heard the last few words of our conversation. "I heard one of them say that you was prob'ly horseback riding alongside the road on the north," he said.

In another minute old Goose Neck had finished his coffee, and he called the all aboard. I stood up, much as it hurt me to do it, and I stopped him and Ash Face. "Listen," I said, "when we get back to Asininity, I don't want neither one of you to say nothing about all this. Far as you know, I never got the message about old Van Pelt stealing that money, and he just got away with it. That's all."

Goose Neck looked at Ash Face, and Ash Face give a shrug. "We don't know nothing," Goose Neck said.

"Good," I said, and I picked up my coat and my boots, and I followed them on out to the stagecoach where it was ready to go and a-waiting.

Chapter Seventeen

We got back to Asininity without nothing of no note happening along the way, and whenever I final and at last clumb down out of that goddamned stagecoach, I was still in my stocking feet and limping something awful. I was met right there and near overwhelmed immediate by Lillian, the kid, Bonnie, Happy, Peester, and old Markham, the goddamned bank president. My goddamned feet was all-fired tender from all that abuse they had suffered that all I wanted to do was to just get myself to a chair or a bed or something. "Where's Loren Van Pelt and the bank's money?" the damned banker shouted.

"Did you turn old Jug in?" Happy asked me.

"Poppa. Poppa," the kid hollered.

"Pick up your baby, Barjack," Lillian snapped. "He wants you."

"Goddamn you all," I shouted. "Shut the hell up."

Well, by God, they did, and I couldn't hardly believe it. Anyhow, when it got good and quiet, I said real low and calm, "Now I'm going on over to the Hooch House and get myself down into a tub of hot water to soak for a spell. I've had a hell of a trip. My muscles and bones is been whipped all to hell. I want some good whiskey, and I want me a steak dinner brought over to me in the tub. Once I'm in the hot water and have et, you all can come in one at a time to ask me your goddamn questions, but till then I ain't saying a goddamn word more to anyone."

"I'll get the tub ready," said Bonnie, and she tuck off running toward Harvey's just a-shaking all her bountifulness with each step. I give Lillian the hardest kind of look I knowed how to give, and she said, "I'll get the steak started." She jerked the kid by his hand and flounced off toward the White Owl. That just left old banker Markham, Peester, and Happy. I put one arm around old Peester's shoulders and the other around the banker's, and I said, "Let's go," and I made them two damn near carry me on over to the Hooch House and then on upstairs to a room. The tub was already setting there in the middle of the floor, and I chased them two bastards off. Then I dropped my old coat and my boots on the floor and fell back on the bed. I'd a gone to sleep right then, but only I was too tired to sleep, and I was still hurting too damn much.

In just a little while old Bonnie had my bath drawed, and then she pulled me up from the bed, helped me get nekkid, and held on to me while I stepped over into that hot, soapy water. I sank down deep in it all the way up to my chin, and Bonnie give me a tumbler full of whiskey. In just a few more minutes, Lillian come in with my dinner on a plate, and I tuck to it like a dog to a bone. When I final finished it up, Bonnie poured me another tumbler full of whiskey. I tell you what. I had been thinking, as you know, about running out on Asininity and ever'one in it, but setting in that tub of hot water, I was never so happy to be back anywhere as I was to be back in Asininity just at that there precise moment in the whole history of time.

I had old Bonnie fetch me a lit-up cigar, and I leaned my head back against the edge of the tub and puffed away. Ever'now and then, I tuck that cigar out of my mouth and slurped some whiskey out of my glass. Bonnie commenced to scrubbing me down, and I just laid there and let her. Ever'thing sure felt good. In a while, though, there was a knocking on the damn door. "Who is it?" Bonnie screeched.

The answer come through the door, "It's Happy." Bonnie give me a quizzical kind of look, and I said, "Let him on in."

She yelled out, "Come on in, Happy."

Old Happy come into the room holding his hat in his hands. "You all right, Barjack?" he asked me.

"That there was mighty questionable up till a few minutes ago," I said, "but I think that right now I can say that I reckon I'll live a while yet."

"Welcome home," he said, and I didn't say nothing back to that. "Barjack?" he said. "Did you deliver old Jug to that marshal in Denver?"

I thought about my scheme and all I had did. "I delivered him up, all right," I said. "If you look in my inside coat pocket, you'll find the papers all signed by that U.S. Marshal Boles. Ever'thing's done up all legal and proper."

Happy looked around, found my coat on the floor where I'd dropped it, and picked it up. The first thing he seen was them two sticks of dynamite. "Barjack?" he said.

"Never mind them things," I said. "Check the pocket on the other side." He did and he found the papers. He also come up with the five hundred dollars the bank in Denver had give me to reimburse Asininity for the reward money we had paid to Happy. He held it up for me to see. "Lay that green stuff on the table over there," I said. "That's the town's money. I expect old Peester will be along soon enough wanting to know about it and get his damn sticky fingers on it." Happy done what I told him to do.

"Barjack?" he said again. "Did you stick around out there in Denver for the hanging?"

"There wasn't no hanging," I said. "Old Jug's brother is Snake Eyes Marlin. You didn't know that, did you?"

"I never," Happy said, and his jaw was hanging down in surprise.

"Well, he is," I told him, "and the son of a bitch attacked me all along the way a-trying to save his brother. Eventual poor old Jug got hisself in the way of some of them bullets. He was killed dead, and in a while he just got too stinky to carry along thataway, so I had to cut off his head and deliver that to the

227

marshal in order to get our money reimbursed."

"Damn," said Happy, twisting his old face all up like as if he'd bit into a persimmon, "you cut off his head?"

"Had to," I said. "By then, he didn't feel nothing. It's all in them papers. Take them on over to the office and file them away now."

Happy went on out then, a-shaking his head as he walked. Old Bonnie tuck the tale of the head cutting pretty good, though. She just kept on a-scrubbing me all over, and I sure was enjoying it. She was too. I could tell. Pretty damn soon Peester come in, and he got the five hundred, and it wasn't long after him that the damn banker come on in. "Did you receive my telegram?" he said, real demanding-like. I tuck a drink, and then I looked at him.

"What telegram?" I said. I thought he was going to faint dead away right then and there. He put a hand up over his forehead and he sort of fell down into a chair with his head hanging. "Oh, no," he said. "No. I'm ruined."

"What the hell's the matter with you?" I asked him. 'Course, actual, I knowed damn well what it was a-killing his worthless soul.

"Van Pelt robbed the bank," he said. "As soon as we found out, we sent a telegram hoping to catch you, so you could arrest him and recover the money. What happened? What went wrong? You were on the same stagecoach with him and all that money. What happened?"

"Damned if I know," I said. "I never got no telegram. We can send out wires to Denver. That's where he got off the stage. That U.S. Marshal Boles out there is a pretty good man. Maybe they'll catch old Pelty for us before he spends too much of your money."

Well, old Markham moaned and groaned something fierce, and he come close to crying out loud like a baby. Bonnie final just had to run him off, telling him that there wasn't nothing more I could do for him just then. Then Lillian come in looking real haughty. She had left the kid somewheres, I expect with old Myrtle. She seen Bonnie still scrubbing on me, and she give Bonnie a real cold look. 'Course, old Bonnie's scrubbing hand was deep in the water in a kind of suspicious position. Then Lillian turned the same look on me. "If you're quite finished with your bath," she said, "will you be coming home?"

"Lillian," I said, "I'll be coming home when I'm goddamned good and ready, and I don't want to see no more of them wintry kind of looks from you, neither. Goddamn it, woman, I ain't never laid a unkind hand on you yet, but if you don't change your high-and-mighty nagging ways you got aimed against me, I swear, by God, I will knock you right down on your ass. You got that?"

She got it, 'cause she never talked back. She just turned around and headed for the door, but before she walked on out, I said, "And when I do get home, I don't want that kid yelling around, and I don't want him throwing things in the house. You ride herd on him, and you do it good. And, hey, woman. Send me a clean suit of clothes over here. I might just decide I want to get out of here and get dressed again."

She paused a second, drawed herself up real tall, and walked on out. Bonnie let out the air she had been holding in her lungs. "Barjack," she said, "she's liable to be waiting for you at home with a cocked six-gun."

I tuck me a drink, and I said, "All I got to say is that if she ain't done what I told her to do, then she'd better damn well pull the trigger." I tipped up the glass then and drained it, and I held it out toward Bonnie. "Would you fill this son of a bitch back up for me, sweet ass?" I said. She smiled real nice and kind and tuck the glass. After she'd poured it back full, she give it to me again.

"When your clean suit gets over here," she said, "you going to get dressed and go home?"

"I ain't in no hurry to go home," I said, and I put a hand behind her head and pulled her face down to my own and give her a real slobbery kiss. I had been soaking for a while, and I was beginning to feel considerable better. And after Bonnie scrubbing me all over the way she done, I was also starting to feel somewhat frisky, if you get my meaning. In fact, whenever she started to pull away from me, I didn't just only hang on, I pulled back, and pretty soon she come falling over the edge of the tub right into the water with me. She screamed and made a big splash, and I just cuddled her to me and played with her big tits.

"I think you'd ought to get out of them wet clothes," I told her, and so I commenced to helping her do just that. She didn't mind none either, and pretty quick we was both setting nekkid together in that tub of water, and we done the fun and naughty act right there a-sloshing water all over the floor. Now, that was a new one on me, I can tell you, and it caused all kinds of waves, but it was sure enough fun. Whenever we was done, we got out of the tub, and Bonnie got a towel and dried us both off. Just about then there was a knock on the door. It was old Aubrey bringing my clean clothes up to me, and I give silent but profuse thanks to the great God above that Lillian hadn't brung them up her own self.

Bonnie had the towel wrapped around her, and she just opened the door a crack in order to allow Aubrey to hand that stuff in to her. She hung them up on the wall, and then she come back over to me, and I unwrapped her, and we clumb into the bed together and commenced to playing around some more. Eventual we just laid back to relax some, and she said, "I missed you, Barjack. I'm glad you're home."

I said, "Have you been playing around with old Happy while I was gone?"

She said, "Not all that much, sweetie. He gets too embarrassed, and besides, he ain't near as much fun as you are. No one is. Whenever I'm with someone else, I always think about you."

Hell, I decided to let it go at that. I smooched her some to let her know that I appreciated what she had said about me. Then I set up on the edge of the bed. "Well, I reckon I better get my clean clothes on and get my old tired ass on over to the marshaling office," I said. "I've been gone for quite a spell, and old Happy might have made a mess of ever'thing. He never had to do no paperwork before, you know."

231

Bonnie got up and fetched my clothes over to me, and I got full dressed, except that once I had my clean socks on, I couldn't hardly bring myself to pull them goddamn boots back on my poor tender feet. "Throw them goddamn boots out," I said to Bonnie. I picked up my coat, tuck the dynamite sticks out of the pocket, and checked all the other pockets. There were a couple of cigars, which I retrieved. Then I held the coat out and said, "This too." I put the blowsticks and the cigars in the inside pocket of my fresh coat, and I got up to head on over to the office.

But I was walking in my sock feet, and I was walking slow and easy, like as if I was walking on a sheet of glass what I didn't want to break, or I was walking across a creaky floor, and I didn't want to make no noise. I walked on down the stairs, and I was wondering how come I had never before noticed how many of them there was, and I made it across the big main room of the Hooch House, on out the door, down the sidewalk and final on over to my office all that same real careful way I had started out, and folks on the street was really watching me too. I seen them. I wanted to say something to them, but I never.

In the office, I found Happy a-setting behind my desk just like it was his own. "You can give me back my chair," I told him, and he jumped up and moved out of the way.

"I was just filing them papers away," he said. I minced my way on around behind the desk and then set down. I heaved a long sigh of relief as the weight come off my feet again at last.

"Happy," I said, "run your ass over and get that

goddamned boot maker to come over here and measure me up for a new pair of boots. Tell him to hurry
it up, too." Well, Happy run on out of there, and I
pulled open my desk drawers to see how much damage he had done while I was gone. I was surprised to
find out that everything was just right where it had
ought to be. Even my whiskey bottle and tumbler was
still where I had left them in the middle right-hand
desk drawer. I brung them out and poured me some.

Just then Happy come back with the boot maker,
and the boot maker measured me all up. He promised
me a new pair of boots by the same time the next
day. "Real soft and cozy," he said.

I said, "They better be," and he went on his way.
Then I told Happy to go saddle up my horse and fetch
him on down to me at the office. I sure wasn't fixing
to walk one step more than I absolute had to. By the
time I had finished my glass of whiskey and poured
myself a fresh one, old Happy was back again.

"He's right outside, Barjack," he said.

"Take over," I said. "I'm going home."

I got up and tippy-toed on out to the street and
managed to get myself up into the saddle. On my
slow ride over to my house, I was wondering just
what I would be facing when I got there, but I was
determined that things was going to be different
around me from that time on out. I seen a few folks
along the way and howdied them, and I also seen that
ever'one of them looked at my sock feet in the stir-
rups as I rode by them. They never said nothing,
though, and I never did either. Maybe I'd let ever'one
know the whole story someday. Maybe I wouldn't.

Robert J. Conley

Either way, I figgered, it was none of their goddamned business.

At the hitch rail in front of my house, I did manage to pull the saddle off my horse, but I left the poor son of a bitch standing there at the rail, and I went on inside. Well, by God, old Lillian met me right there at the door, and she was wearing a flimsy night thing that I hadn't saw for some time. She sure did look good to me, and she was smelling real sweet too, but I made myself stay tough. "Where's the kid at?" I asked her.

"I put him to bed," she said. "He's asleep. You do look a little better now. Do you feel better?"

"I'm some better," I said, "but I had me a hell of a trip. I'm plumb wore out, and I'm sore all over."

I kind of wanted to tell her the whole sorry story. I hadn't yet told no one. Goose Neck and Ash Face was the only ones who knowed most of it, and they even didn't know just exactly how old Pelty had actual got away from me. But I decided to just keep it all to myself, at least for the time being. Lillian surprised the hell out of me just then. She reached her soft, smooth arms right around my neck and give me a real sweet kiss on the lips. When she backed off, she said, "You want a drink?"

Well, I ain't never been knowed to say no to that question, so she went and poured me one. While she was doing that, I set myself down on the couch in our living room. She brung the drink to me over there. It was whiskey in a tumbler, just the way I like it. She knowed that. I tuck the drink, and she set down beside me and put an arm around my shoulders.

While I drank, she give me little nibbling kisses all over the side of my face.

Pretty soon it come to remind me of our earliest times together whenever it was so good and I still thought that she was the finest thing that had ever come into my life. I guess that all it tuck to fix things up was me yelling at her and threatening her like I done. I wondered what I would a done if she hadn't paid no attention to my threat. I don't really believe that I could ever have brung myself to hit her like I had said I would. No matter how bad things had got between us, Lillian was still the goddamndest lady I had ever knowed. I guess I might have run out on her or run her off, but I don't believe I could ever have done her no harm.

Anyhow, I went and put that glass down, and we really got to loving on each other, and I final broke loose just a bit, and I said, before I even knowed just what the hell it was that I was fixing to say, I had done went and said, "Lillian, darlin', I guess I ain't showed it much for a spell, but goddamn it, I reckon I love you." She smiled at me, and then she mimicked my way of talking, and she said, "Barjack, I reckon I do love you too. And things're going to be different around here from now on."

Chapter Eighteen

I'll tell you what. I woke up the next morning feeling like I was on top of the whole goddamned world. Hell, I hadn't felt better since I had first got hold of Lillian. Yes, indeed, I thought that I was king of the whole world, till I swung my poor feet off the bed and put them down on the floor. Goddamn, did that ever hurt like blue blazing fire. I thought I had stepped down into some of old Harp's brimstone. Then I thought that I was sniffling some coffee, and I couldn't hardly believe it. I hadn't smelled no coffee in my own house for months. I was setting there on the edge of the bed trying to talk myself into standing up on them poor abused feet of mine, when Lillian peeked in the door with a sweet smile on her lovely face. "Coffee?" she said.

"Damn right," I said, and she come on back in

bringing me coffee on a tray. She put it down on the table there beside the bed, and then she bent over and lifted up my feet, laying them back on the bed. I laid back, and she put two big fluffy pillers under my head and kind of set me up. Then she handed me the cup full of hot black coffee. I sipped at it. Damn, it was good. Then she offered me some breakfast, which I, of course, accepted, and in a couple more minutes she brung that in to me and served me in bed. Well, I did feel like the king of Siam or some damn place.

I was just about to tie into them eggs and ham and taters and such when the kid stepped into the room. He was dressed up all proper, and he had his hands folded behind his back. He stopped just inside the door and looked at me. I glared back at him, waiting for him to do something awful like run and jump right in the big middle of me and my breakfast, or bring a ball out from behind his back and throw it at my head, but he never.

"Good morning, Poppa," he said. "I'm glad you're home. I missed you."

I still didn't trust the little bastard, so I just kept a-glaring at him and I kind of grunted back at him. Lillian said, "That's a good boy. Run along, now." And by God, he did. Well, there was wonders a-working somewhere. I even thought for just a minute there that maybe it was all because I got old Harp to baptize me in that stagecoach. I'd heard folks say that if you give yourself to God good things will follow. 'Course, old Harp wasn't much of a goddamned preacher, but maybe that didn't have nothing to do with it. After all, he had splashed water on my head in the name of the Lord.

Well, I decided that I just didn't know what it was that I owed my good fortune to, but I was just going to lay back and enjoy it, that's all. I finished that good breakfast what my own sweet Lillian had fixed up for me with her own lovely hands, and she brung me some more coffee. Pretty soon I had to get up to go out back to the john, and I thought that my poor feet was going to kill me on that normally short trip, but I made it out there and back, and I got myself back into bed. Whenever my Lillian figgered out what it was that was paining me so, she washed my feet and dried them off and then put some kind of salve or ointment or something on them, and they did feel some better after that.

I made up my mind that I was just going to lay there in bed all damn day, as long as my Lillian was being so good to me. I was scared that it was too good to last, and I meant to take full advantage of it while I could. By and by, she come back in and told me that she had sent the kid off with Myrtle, and it was just me and her at home all alone. She tuck off her robe she was wearing and crawled back into bed with me, and damned if we didn't have ourselfs another fine old time in there. Whenever she had final beat me down, and I just couldn't keep up with her no more, she got up and lit me a cigar and fetched me in a tumbler full of whiskey.

Well, if I had thought that I felt good whenever I first woke up, I just didn't know yet. I had come from being the King of Siam to being the goddamn emperor of all of entire Asia and Europe and maybe the whole damn world. I meant to just lay around in bed all day, but after a while, I just couldn't stand it no longer. I got myself up, walking kind of tenderly, and I got dressed. I had on my suit and hat, my Colts and my socks, but no boots. I told Lillian that I just couldn't afford to ignore my job no more, and I had to go on down to the office. She allowed as how she understood that, and anyhow, she kind of was thinking that maybe she had ought to go check on how things was going at the White Owl.

Well, I offered to drive her in the buggy, and she thought that I was being mighty gentlemanly, but the real reason I wanted to do that was because my sock feet would be hid from the gawking public if I was a-driving the buggy. She hitched it on up, and I throwed the saddle back on my riding horse. Lillian brought the buggy around, and I tied the saddle horse on behind. Then I clumb up beside Lillian and tuck the reins away from her. I drove us on into town and let her off at the White Owl. Then I drove on over to my marshaling office.

I looked both ways down the street and didn't see no one too close by, so I got down and into the office as quick as I could on my tender feet. Happy jumped up from behind my desk as I stepped in. "Morning, Marshal," he said. "You get all rested up?" I went on around behind my desk and set down. The seat was warm, so I knowed that Happy had been setting there for a while.

"Why the hell don't you get on out of here and

check over the town?" I said. "How come you think you're getting paid? To just set here?"

He headed for the door, but I called out after him just as he was about to go on through. "While you're at it," I said, "take care of them horses out there for me."

He said, "Yes, sir," and then he went on out. I settled back in my chair and felt pretty good. Even if someone was to come in to see me, he wouldn't be able to see my feet while I was back there behind my desk. I went through the files for a spell to see what kind of papers old Happy might have stuck in there while I was gone, and it didn't seem to me like he had done nothing. I did find where he had filed the papers from Denver under "J." I guess it was for Jug.

Well, I shuffled papers till I couldn't stand no more of it, and then I went and poured myself a glass full of whiskey. By the time I had drunk down about half of it, old Happy come on back in. "Everything's quiet out there, Barjack," he said. "Your horses is both down to the stable." I didn't say nothing for a minute or so, and he said, "Is there something else you want me to do?"

I said, "Yeah. Go check on my boots."

Well, he went on out grumbling, and I was about to go crazy feeling trapped right there behind my own desk. I wanted to go on down to the Hooch House or even over to the White Owl. I wanted some company besides just old Happy, and I wanted my goddamned boots. But whenever Happy come back he said they was only just halfway done. He said the boot maker was working away on them as hard and as fast as he could, but he was going to be at it for just as long as what he had told me.

I offered a drink to old Happy, but he said that it was way too early in the day for him, so I just had myself another one, and I lit me a cigar. Whenever I went to fetch a cigar out of my pocket, I felt them two sticks of dynamite still there where I had put them, and I thought that I had ought to take them out and put them away somewheres or get rid of them or something, but I never. Not just then. I figgered I'd get around to it eventual.

So we just set there a-talking, and old Happy asked me to tell him all about the troubles I'd had getting old Jug delivered proper, even though I'd actual only delivered his head, so I told him about the guns planted in the outhouses and the fights with old Snake Eyes's gang along the way, and I embellished it all somewhat for old Happy's sake. I knowed he liked a good story. Well, when I final run down, it was damn near noon, and I sent old Happy over to the White Owl to fetch us a couple·of fine steak dinners back to the office. He grumbled something about not knowing that a deputy marshal wasn't nothing but a errand boy, but he went all right. 'Special when I told him that I thought that meals what had to be et in the office while we was on marshaling business should be paid for by the town. "Tell Lillian I said to send the bill on over," I said, and he went on.

We had us a good meal there in the office, and I signed the bill that Lillian had sent over and stuck it in the drawer where I kept all my documents what would be sent over to old Peester's office for the paying out of them. Then I drunk myself some more whiskey, a little bit, and final on toward the late afternoon, the old boot maker at last brought me my new boots. And oh they was soft and nice. And they fit just right. I slipped them things on, and they didn't hardly even hurt my feet, which was still plenty tender. I paid for them right out of my pocket and thanked the feller kindly for his work. He went off happy, and he left me that way too. That's the way business ought to be done.

"Happy," I said, standing up, "let's us walk over to the Hooch House." I wanted to test them new boots. Well, my feet was still tender, but it didn't hurt no more to walk in them fine new boots than what it had to walk barefoot. I went slow and made old Happy stay right alongside me, but I did walk all the way over there. We got into Harvey's and set us down at a table with old Bonnie and got us some drinks all around. Bonnie asked me how things was at home with Lillian, and I told her they had never been better.

"I'm glad to hear that," she said. "You know, Barjack, when you first threw me over for Lillian, it really pissed me off, but me and her has got to be pretty good friends now. I'm glad things're patched up."

I reached over and patted her on her pudgy little hand. " 'Special since me and you has remained such good friends, huh?" I said. She punched me on the shoulder, but it was a light and good-natured punch, so I leaned over and kissed her on the cheek. Then, when she wasn't looking, I wiped my lips on my sleeve, 'cause I was afraid that I might have got some of her makeup on me. I tuck out a cigar and fired it up, and then I gulped me some more whiskey down. As I was lowering my tumbler down, I happened to glance up toward the door, and I like to have dropped my glass at what I seen. There was old Jug just stepped inside the door, and he was a-looking right at me. I put my glass down and stood up. I wanted to stop him before anyone else, mainly Happy, got a good look at him, but I was too late.

"Hello, Barjack," Jug said.

"Howdy, Jug," I said.

"Barjack," said Happy, more than some astonished at what he was a-seeing, "That's Jug Marlin. You said you cut his head off."

"That ain't Jug Marlin, Happy," I said. "He sure looks like old Jug Marlin, I'll give you that, and what's more, that ain't the most coincidence about the thing. This here is old Jug Martin. I met him on my way to Denver."

"I'd swear that there's Jug Marlin," Happy said.

"Ain't you ever heard of a man having a double?" I said. "Hell, once I seen a man what looked just like you, the spitting image. I walked right up to him and looked him in the face and said howdy to him and called him by name, and he just looked at me like he thought I was crazy. Besides, you seen the paperwork. You doubting not just only my word but the word of United States Marshal Boles to boot?"

"Well, no," Happy said. "I reckon not."

I walked on over to old Jug and give him a look. "What brings you to town, Mr. Martin?" I said.

"I got some friends outside," he said, a-grinning, "and we brung you something."

I tuck a puff on my cigar, then follered him outside. There, all strung out in a line and facing me, was old Snake Eyes and all that was left of his gang. There was six of them, counting Snake Eyes, and with old Jug what was still standing there beside me, there was seven. I seen another man on a horse back kind of behind Snake Eyes, but I couldn't see him too good. "Barjack," Snake Eyes said, "here's your prisoner." He pulled on a rope and the horse and rider behind him come forward, and I seen that it was old Van Pelt.

"Well," I said, "hello there, Pelty. Climb on down."

"I can't," he said. "I'm tied to the saddle."

I looked over my shoulder to yell at Happy and get him out there with me, but whenever I turned I seen him right there behind me. "Happy," I said, "get old Pelty down and take him to jail and lock him up."

Happy went out to do what I had told him to do, and whenever he slipped past Snake Eyes, he kind of brushed into something hanging there at Snake Eyes's side, and I seen that it was my valise. "I see you brung my baggage back to me, too," I said. "I'm obliged. Just toss it over here."

"Why, sure," he said. He jerked it loose and tossed it at me. It landed right on the board sidewalk in front of my new boots. I picked it up and jerked it open, and there was two bottles of whiskey and my extra clothes. There wasn't no money. I seen that I had myself a problem right then.

"Where's the rest of what was in there?" I asked him.

"Why, Barjack," Snake Eyes said, "what else was

in there? You missing a pair of long johns or something?"

"Damn it, Snake Eyes," I said. "You know what I'm talking about."

"If you was to invite me down to have a drink," he said, "we might could talk about it. We had us a long ride."

"Come on down, boys," I said. "Welcome to Harvey's Hooch House."

I picked up my valise, turned and went back inside, and set down at a empty table. Old Jug set down on my left-hand side, and when Snake Eyes come in, he set by my right. When the other five come in, I said, "Belly up to the bar, boys. The drinks is on me." They all did that, and then I tuck a bottle out of my valise for the three of us there at the table. I opened her up and tuck a drink. Then I slid the bottle to Snake Eyes. He tuck a drink and passed it on over to Jug. We didn't talk none for a spell, and when old Aubrey had served all them boys at the bar, he brung over some glasses. I poured them all full for the three of us at the table. Happy stepped back in just then, and he just stepped to one side and stood there by the door a-watching.

"All right, Snake Eyes," I said, "where the hell's all that there bank money?"

"Barjack," he said, "I brought your bank robber back to you, because of what you done for my brother. Ain't that enough?"

"It's something," I said, "but it ain't enough."

He leaned over close to me then, and he said in a

real low voice, "You want some of it? You want a share? Hell, I can give you a share."

"I want it all," I said. "It's going back to the bank. Hell, a share of it's mine anyhow. I kept my goddamned money in that bank."

"Tell you what," he said. "You tell me how much you had in the bank, and I'll give that back to you. Then we'll give you an even share of what's left. I can't do no better than that. That's fair. It's more than fair."

"It ain't no deal," I said. "The money has got to go back to the bank. Where the hell you got it hid?"

"Barjack," he said, "hell, I don't want to fight you. What you got here? One deputy? That one that took Van Pelt off to jail? There's seven of us. You can't win. Listen. That's more money than I ever seen at one time in my whole life. Things're getting hot for us around these parts. Hell, we're wanted all over. I mean to take that money and get us out of the country. We can all live high and free. I ain't going to let you have it, Barjack. Use your head. I'm offering you a hell of a deal."

I tuck myself a drink, and he did too. So far old Jug hadn't said nothing. He was just watching the two of us and listening. I put down my glass, and I said, "I appreciate it, Snake Eyes, but you got to understand my position here. I'm the town marshal. I'm a businessman too. You see this here place, this Hooch House? Hell, it's mine. And did you get a look at that fine eating place across the street, the White Owl Supper Club? That's mine too. I'm a respected citizen of this here town, and I can't cut no deal with the likes of you. I don't mean no insult by that, but I reckon you know what I mean."

Snake Eyes heaved a sigh. "I sure don't want to fight you," he said. "I'd hate to have to kill you after what you done for us. But I reckon me and the boys'll just mount up and ride out of town. If you and that deputy of yours are fool enough to start shooting at the seven of us, well, it'll be you that started it. Not me."

"Hell," I said, and I tuck a puff of my cigar, "that's likely the way it'll play out, but till that happens, let's have us some more drinks together."

"You ain't going to get me drunk, Barjack," Snake Eyes said.

"Hell, I know that," I told him. "I been drinking all day already. Hell, I'll be drunk long before you will. Have another one with me, will you?" And just as I said that, I went and put my right arm around his shoulder and give him a kind of hug.

"Yeah," he said, "I'll have another one. There ain't no hurry."

As he was pouring his drink, I tuck the cigar out of my mouth with my left hand, and I slipped it under my coat. I had to feel around a bit for the fuse of one of them sticks, but I found it all right, and just the instant it started to fizz, I clamped my right arm hard around old Snake Eyes's head and pulled him in close to me. He hauled out his Colt with his right hand, but I pulled my coat open, and that fuse was fizzing right under his nose. "Throw it on the floor," I said, and he did. "You too, Jug," I said. Jug pulled out his own side arm and dropped it to the floor.

"Now," I said, "you tell them others to drop their guns."

"You're bluffing, Barjack," he said.

"You'll never know it if I ain't," I said. "Tell them."

"Boys," he called out, "drop your guns. Do it now."

They all did, and then I said to Happy, "Go pick them guns all up and toss them behind the bar." Happy done that real quick, 'cause he seen what I had fizzing in my pocket too. Bonnie and Aubrey and the customers got up screaming and squealing and run outside. "All right, Snake Eyes," I said, "where the hell's the money?"

"You're bluffing," he said again. "You ain't going to sit here and get yourself blown all to hell with me."

"I'm a stubborn son of a bitch," I said. "I want that money."

For a spell there all Snake Eyes done was to just watch that fuse fizz right under his nose. His slitty little eyes was open real wide, I can tell you. I didn't let on none to no one around me, but I was nervous as hell too. I was sweating, and I was scared that I might piss my pants. I didn't know for sure just how long that there fuse would burn before it blowed. Final old Snake Eyes couldn't take it no longer. "In my saddlebags," he said. "In my saddlebags. Let me go."

"Just set still," I said. "Happy, go out there and check his saddlebags."

Happy went out, and Snake Eyes said, "Damn it, Barjack. I told you. Let me go before that thing blows up."

"Set still," I said.

Happy come back in and said, "It's there all right, Barjack."

I said, "All right, Happy, go behind the bar and get old Aubrey's shotgun." Then I told them at the bar to bunch up real close together, and Happy come back out from behind the bar. He pointed that scattergun right at the middle of them five. I eased up on Snake Eyes, and I said, "Get over there with the rest of them. You too, Jug." Snake Eyes broke loose as fast as he could, and him and Jug both moved over there to huddle up with their buddies at the bar. I stood up and walked over to stand by Happy.

"Barjack," Snake Eyes hollered, "get rid of that damn dynamite."

I tuck the gun out of Happy's hands, and then I handed him the lit stick. "Get rid of this," I told him. First off he looked at it with wide eyes, and then he turned and run out the door like hell. "Boys," I said, "we'll be walking on down to the jailhouse in just a minute." Then we heard the blast, and it shuck the glasses and bottles behind the bar. A couple of the Snake Eyes boys pissed their pants, and old Jug, he messed his. "Snake Eyes," I said, "don't get no smart ideas. This scattergun will take out you and two or three more with just one blast, and it's got two barrels."

Happy come back in then. He was staggering a little, and he was covered with dirt. He had some grass and twigs and stuff stuck in his hair and on his shirt and britches. He sure looked rough. "Goddamn," said Snake Eyes.

"Happy," I said, "get outside and pull your Colt.

Robert J. Conley

Cover these bastards from the front. I'll be right behind them with this shotgun. We're marching them to the jailhouse."

Well, we locked them all up all right, and then I tuck the money back to old Markham, and he was so tickled I thought for a minute he was going to kiss me. I got out of there as fast as I could. So the money was back, the bank robber was in jail, and so was the whole damn Snake Eyes gang. I felt pretty good about all that, and so I got four bottles of whiskey and tuck them over to the jailhouse. I give Snake Eyes and them three bottles, and me and Happy set out in the office and commenced to get drunk with them. Hell, even old Pelty drunk hisself some of it.

So it come about that I was even a bigger hero than I had been before, and I had even got peace at home with my own little family. Pelty and Snake Eyes and all them was eventual tried and sent to the pen, and a silly-ass little writer come to town and writ me up for some magazine. I figgered that I was well set up for the rest of my life, and it was all due to that time that I had been so bored with life in Asininity that I had just gone and broke loose.

Barjack

ROBERT J. CONLEY

Barjack isn't a big man. But he is ornery. When he comes to the town of Asininity he doesn't plan on staying long. But that is before he runs into a bit of trouble in the saloon. When the fighting is over and Barjack is the only one still standing, the head of the town council offers him the job of town marshal. To Barjack it is just another job, as good as any other. Trouble is, it is a job that makes him enemies—bad enemies like the Bensons. A while back Barjack rounded up the five Benson brothers for murder and rustling. One brother was hanged, the others sent to the pen. And now the surviving brothers are out and coming back to town with one purpose in mind . . . to make Barjack pay.

___4687-3 $4.50 US/$5.50 CAN

Dorchester Publishing Co., Inc.
P.O. Box 6640
Wayne, PA 19087-8640

Please add $1.75 for shipping and handling for the first book and $.50 for each book thereafter. NY, NYC, and PA residents, please add appropriate sales tax. No cash, stamps, or C.O.D.s. All orders shipped within 6 weeks via postal service book rate. Canadian orders require $2.00 extra postage and must be paid in U.S. dollars through a U.S. banking facility.

Name_____
Address_____
City_____ State_____ Zip_____
I have enclosed $ _____ in payment for the checked book(s).
Payment <u>must</u> accompany all orders. ❑ Please send a free catalog.

THE ACTOR

ROBERT J. CONLEY

Bluford Steele had always been an outsider until he found his calling as an actor. Instead of being just another half-breed Cherokee with a white man's education, he can be whomever he chooses. But when the traveling acting troupe he is with arrives in the wild, lawless town of West Riddle, the man who rules the town with an iron fist forces them to perform. Then he steals all the proceeds. Steele is determined to get the money back, even if it means playing the most dangerous role of his life—a cold-blooded gunslinger ready to face down any man who gets in his way.

___4498-6 $4.50 US/$5.50 CAN

Dorchester Publishing Co., Inc.
P.O. Box 6640
Wayne, PA 19087-8640

Please add $1.75 for shipping and handling for the first book and $.50 for each book thereafter. NY, NYC, and PA residents, please add appropriate sales tax. No cash, stamps, or C.O.D.s. All orders shipped within 6 weeks via postal service book rate. Canadian orders require $2.00 extra postage and must be paid in U.S. dollars through a U.S. banking facility.

Name_____
Address_____
City_____State_____Zip_____
I have enclosed $_____ in payment for the checked book(s).
Payment <u>must</u> accompany all orders. ❑ Please send a free catalog.
     CHECK OUT OUR WEBSITE! www.dorchesterpub.com

INCIDENT at BUFFALO CROSSING

ROBERT J. CONLEY

The Sacred Hill. It rose above the land, drawing men to it like a beacon. But the men who came each had their own dreams. There is Zeno Bond, the settler who dreams of land and empire. There is Mat McDonald, captain of the steamship *John Hart*, heading the looming war between the Spanish and the Americans. And there is Walker, the Cherokee warrior called by a vision he cannot deny—a vision of life, death...and destiny.

___4396-3 $4.50 US/$5.50 CAN

Dorchester Publishing Co., Inc.
P.O. Box 6640
Wayne, PA 19087-8640

Please add $1.75 for shipping and handling for the first book and $.50 for each book thereafter. NY, NYC, and PA residents, please add appropriate sales tax. No cash, stamps, or C.O.D.s. All orders shipped within 6 weeks via postal service book rate. Canadian orders require $2.00 extra postage and must be paid in U.S. dollars through a U.S. banking facility.

Name_____
Address_____
City_____State_____Zip_____
I have enclosed $_____ in payment for the checked book(s).
Payment <u>must</u> accompany all orders. ❑ Please send a free catalog.
     CHECK OUT OUR WEBSITE! www.dorchesterpub.com

BACK TO MALACHI

ROBERT J. CONLEY
THREE-TIME SPUR
AWARD-WINNER

Charlie Black is a young half-breed caught between two worlds. He is drawn to the promise of the white man's wealth, but torn by his proud heritage as a Cherokee. Charlie's pretty young fiancée yearns for the respectability of a Christian marriage and baptized children. But Charlie can't forsake his two childhood friends, Mose and Henry Pathkiller, who live in the hills with an old full-blooded Indian named Malachi. When Mose runs afoul of the law, Charlie has to choose between the ways of his fiancée and those of his friends and forefathers. He has to choose between surrender and bloodshed.

___4277-0 $3.99 US/$4.99 CAN

Dorchester Publishing Co., Inc.
P.O. Box 6640
Wayne, PA 19087-8640

Please add $1.75 for shipping and handling for the first book and $.50 for each book thereafter. NY, NYC, and PA residents, please add appropriate sales tax. No cash, stamps, or C.O.D.s. All orders shipped within 6 weeks via postal service book rate. Canadian orders require $2.00 extra postage and must be paid in U.S. dollars through a U.S. banking facility.

Name_____
Address_____
City_____State_____Zip_____
I have enclosed $_____ in payment for the checked book(s).
Payment <u>must</u> accompany all orders. ❏ Please send a free catalog.

MOVING ON

JANE CANDIA COLEMAN

Jane Candia Coleman is a magical storyteller who spins brilliant tales of human survival, hope, and courage on the American frontier, and nowhere is her marvelous talent more in evidence than in this acclaimed collection of her finest work. From a haunting story of the night Billy the Kid died, to a dramatic account of a breathtaking horse race, including two stories that won the prestigious Spur Award, here is a collection that reveals the passion and fortitude of its characters, and also the power of a wonderful writer.

___4545-1 $4.99 US/$5.99 CAN

Dorchester Publishing Co., Inc.
P.O. Box 6640
Wayne, PA 19087-8640

Please add $1.75 for shipping and handling for the first book and $.50 for each book thereafter. NY, NYC, and PA residents, please add appropriate sales tax. No cash, stamps, or C.O.D.s. All orders shipped within 6 weeks via postal service book rate. Canadian orders require $2.00 extra postage and must be paid in U.S. dollars through a U.S. banking facility.

Name_____
Address_____
City_____ State_____ Zip_____
I have enclosed $_____ in payment for the checked book(s).
Payment <u>must</u> accompany all orders. ☐ Please send a free catalog.
    CHECK OUT OUR WEBSITE! www.dorchesterpub.com

ATTENTION WESTERN CUSTOMERS!

SPECIAL TOLL-FREE NUMBER
1-800-481-9191

*Call Monday through Friday
10 a.m. to 9 p.m.
Eastern Time
Get a free catalogue,
join the Western Book Club,
and order books using your
Visa, MasterCard,
or Discover®*

Leisure
Books

GO ONLINE WITH US AT DORCHESTERPUB.COM